D1355565

EDINBURGH'S ONE O'CLOCK GUN PERIODICAL

One O'Clock Gun

Anthology

With an introduction by R A Jamieson

Wisdom • Industry • Magic

Leamington Books
2010

Contents

Illustrations

By Lucy McKenzie

"Keep your powder dry, mate, for the city we love."
Angus Calder

One O'Clock Gunnery

Edinburgh – the first UNESCO World City of Literature
– where brass and blue plaques, to writers old and new, form a
treasure trail for the faithful to follow – in the footsteps of the
national bard for one; where the main station itself is called
after a novel; where the monument to wizardly Sir Walter
dominates even Christmas, and Allan Ramsay's statue by the
floral clock keys the fine 'New' street of Princes to the 'Old'
town where he lived and worked, to the exotic pink house that
bears his name at the Castle's cheek; where writers have been
drawn, from others parts of Scotland and farther furth than
that for centuries. This wondrous old city, once a great world
hub of publishing, the very inventor of print capitalism, where
millionaire authors now live in rows – if they haven't moved to
Ireland for softer tax laws.

12.59 – the minute before the report. The morning has run
its course, the fine shops have traded. Cash has been taken,
credit issued or refused. Edina sits on its darling seat, rocking
gently back and forth, a shade self-congratulatory at its marvels
– but if there were to be doubts, a look at the crowds will quell
those, for on the Mile, in the Castle, and the Palace – the new
Parliament – seekers from all round the world scrabble after
secrets, poking round fabled history on a ghost-hunt. The Blue
Guides are open, the Rough Guides too, little plastic ponchos
flock from site to site.

The One O'Clock Gun – the crack from the barrel breaks the
day briefly in two, hours before and hours to come. But never
on a Sunday – the one o'clock shot first fired on June 7th 1861
has continued since, six days a week, except during the two
World Wars, punctuating the working week. 'Auld Reekie' is the
echo, that place of soot-blackened walls back before the stone-
cleaning began, when people took their lunchbreak at 1 o'clock,
and the shops and offices closed. Day feels its way down every
close and stair after that, and those for whom the Gun signals
waking emerge to join the morning traders. So distinctively
Edinburgh, that blast from the castle, a reminder from the past
to the present that the armed forces are still there, at the core

of the changing city, defending or occupying, depending on
political viewpoint. And of a time when people reeked too; in
literary terms, of those smoky gatherings in Milne's Bar of the
Little Kremlin crowd, or the Heretics at Sandy Bell's cracking to
the sound of the poetry of the Folk revival.

But a literary city is not made up of a few great achievers, the
unique monuments, the great libraries or universities, however
important they may ultimately become in codifying, harnessing
or housing – it grows from the street up, begins with a widely-
shared aspiration to know, to gather and garner, among a huge
host of individuals who seek each other out in the ferment
of second-hand bookshops and new, readings formal and
informal, by the passing of books between readers, groups and
clubs, the howffs and, these days, the smart continental cafes.
Out of this chaos of text and chatter the occasional star emerges
– but without the ferment, without the chaos, this could not
happen. If Edinburgh is a City of Literature, it is so not just
because of its tradition, but because that ferment continues
– largely unseen or glimpsed in passing, immeasurably diverse,
but humming faintly all the time, the traffic of ideas, of words.

And it is out of just that hum the free publication which shares
its name with the One O'Clock Gun emerges, in the decade
known now as the Noughties, taking the shape of the old
columned broadside, and at first, significantly pseudonymous
– with wandering collogues seeming to echo the Noctes
Ambrosianae between such as 'The Master without Honour',
'The Mademoiselle', 'The Heckler' and so forth.

From the outset, a mixture of the ephemeral with the studied,
caricature of contemporary life with the referencing of Hogg
or Protestant martyrs, of Embra's multi-layered past, the
team, whoever they were, were adept at the snooking of cocks,
spoofery and goofery too, but had amongst them attempted
a grasp of the very balls of the city, as evidenced by this
'Situations Vacant' entry from the columns of the first issue:

'Edinburgh desperately requires a Leader of the Mob, a
position last held by 'General' Joseph Smith (?-1780). The
ideal applicant will be boisterous, energetic, unruly, and

have a wealth of relevant experience in the ancient art of rabble-rousing. Duties will include storming the barriers at Hogmanay, disrupting the Tattoo, and harassing the Council and the Lady Provost. An ability to bang the drum loudly is desirable but not essential, as full training will be given.'

The sense of voices from the Edinburgh that is excluded from its own party – in Hogmanay terms, the unticketed – is a theme throughout the broadsheets. The editor's own 'Commoner's Guide to the New Town Pleasure Gardens' makes this point clearly, and there are many forbidden gardens, metaphorically, which 'Gunprints' tread all over, many toes that they step upon, from the not-so-great-and-good such as the Tory councillor Moira Knox, to contemporary heroes like Ian Rankin and Alexander McCall Smith, and temporary ones such as John 'Smeato' Smeaton. The Scottish Arts Council and the City of Literature too take a pasting here and there, but this is the nature, even a necessity, of a healthy culture – or ego. Edinburgh can laugh at its various selves, can contain opposites – the much-vaunted duality (one of the issues the Gun dubiously addressed).

In time, personalities emerged, as the volumes grew. The editor Craig Gibson was revealed and the hand of Lucy McKenzie signed the illustrations. Its columns became starred with work from such luminaries as Alasdair Gray, Angus Calder and Suhayl Saadi, as well as newer writers such as Peter Burnett, Rodge Glass, Gavin Inglis, Jenny Lindsay and Kirsti Wishart – perched alongside the obviously pseudonymous. It marked the passing of key local personalities such as the poet Sandie Craigie and, in time, Angus Calder himself – who perhaps was the best applicant for the post advertised above in his later years.

Scurrilous, offensive and sometimes downright silly, some may say, yet also well informed and soulfully local, the One O'Clock Gun's free presence in choice outlets throughout Embra is evidence that this literary city is still alive at grassroots level. The mob is out there. And kicking still.

Robert Alan Jamieson
(Edinburgh, 10th December 2009)

Editor's Introduction: Volume I (2004)

Edinburgh's One O'Clock Gun Periodical was launched in February 2004 and traced its origins back to a dining and literary society, the Top Slot Club, which I founded to combat the tedium of academia during my last year at Edinburgh University in 2003. The TSC's avowed intention was to write humorous letters to the Edinburgh Evening News in order to provoke ridiculous debates. Whilst we were remarkably successful in this endeavour, we soon grew bored as the game had become a little too easy and several of us decided that the creation of a literary publication would provide us with a fresh challenge.

We envisaged a free paper that would be distributed around pubs and cafés, in a similar manner to the literature prevalent in coffee houses during the Enlightenment. Our earliest influence was the celebrated and scurrilous C19 publication Blackwood's Edinburgh Magazine, and this was reflected in both the style and content. A simple black and white double-sided broadsheet (cunningly folded) with an antiquated-looking masthead and columns galore was deemed ideal for our needs; it looked striking, was easy to distribute, and was relatively cheap to produce. Many of the earliest contributors, who were Top Slot veterans, adopted what became known as our house style, which will become apparent to the reader of this volume. This rather archaic style of writing had become something of an albatross by the end of the volume but it served its purpose admirably, for it left many readers scratching their heads. Were we a bunch of over-educated jokers or were we serious? Well, we were fond of a chuckle but we were deadly serious and convinced we were on a mission to return quality literature to the taverns gratis, providing an antidote to what we perceived as a culture of literary apathy stalking the Capital. Why else would we have chosen Perturbentur Hostes Nostri! (Confusion to our Enemies!) as our rallying cry? At the very least we stood out from the herd and the public tended to either love us or hate us – no half way houses, to paraphrase a certain C M Grieve...

Although we were determined to attract previously published Scottish writers of merit to the paper, our raison d'être was to provide a platform for the legion of amateur scribes who we believed were out there. We were happy to consider anything for publication, though we made no promises (some of the submissions, written in an attempt at house style, were truly painful and thus rejected), but largely this policy paid off and in this volume the majority of the writers, poets and artists appear in print for the very first time. I hope you enjoy taking this trip down memory lane as much as I do.

Editor's note: Many of the contributors in this volume originally appeared under aliases (one of our many Blackwoodesque in-jokes). I have restored the actual names of these individuals wherever possible.

Craig Gibson

Once Again Into The Festival Of Darkness

or, A Guide To Surviving The Edinburgh Winter In Style

Whighams Nights # 1

Winter is rarely welcomed by anyone in Edinburgh except children (Christmas), tourists (Hogmanay, until recently) and manufacturers of warm clothing. It is greatly feared by SAD sufferers and the elderly, amongst other inhabitants of the capital city, but they do not feature in this tale. Nor indeed do children, tourists, or the aforementioned warm clothing manufacturers, for this tale concerns a group of young Edinburgh citizens who welcomed the winter for their own nefarious purposes. This cabal recognised that whilst the Edinburgh winter was laden with its very own problems and difficulties, these could nevertheless be overcome with a little cunning and romance. In addition to this they were united in their belief that Edinburgh's cultural Renaissance was just around the corner, and needed only to be provoked in some manner or other, for these things do not happen without a catalyst.

The so-called Scottish summer was a fucking damp squib of a joke in the first place and it seemed impossible to get anything done, for even at the slightest hint of sunshine everyone tended to forget the present state of affairs in order to sample a bit of the al fresco lifestyle that they remembered from holidays past. In wintertime, however, Edina became the perfect backdrop for plotting and skulduggery, for as well as having city centre scenery to die for, there still existed the kind of tavern that positively begged to be used for this purpose. Have you ever made your way across the freezing, darkened Capital, the elements no match for your enthusiasm as you know you are about to spend the next few hours in a warm convivial heaven drinking, debating, and plotting just like our forefathers? If so, then you will have no problem agreeing with me that Edinburgh is a very, very entrancing place to be in the depth of winter. This is naturally how our cabal felt, and it is to its members that we must turn our attention, for this is a tale with many voices.

One November evening, in his fashionable Stockbridge riverside flat, the Master without Honour smugly checked his appearance in the mirror for the third time before examining his night's marching rations with military precision. He discovered he was carrying: approx. £7.50 of good hashish; a pipe; 12.5g of tobacco; cigarette papers; £20; a Whighams loyalty card. All were found to be present and correct. Adjusting his eight-panelled county cap to a sporty/ritzy angle he exited the flat briskly. Outside, his Crombie greatcoat dealt efficiently with the bitingly cold wind, and both his face and hands were snug under the scarf/glove combo. As he headed up the hill into the white lights of Moray Place with a grim smile on his face, he briefly considered the fact that he would absolutely fucking hate to be working class ever again.

Meanwhile, down in the Grange, the Historian was likewise putting the finishing touches to his wardrobe. Although a man of many aliases, the Historian suited him best, as Scottish history was his avowed religion – even if he did tend to dress like a Presbyterian lay-preacher. He was not a vain man, and so barely glanced at the cheval mirror in his thoroughly masculine bedroom as he donned his black overcoat. Despite being garbed in a costume that would have made Robert Wringham look like a tart, he was in reality a convivial fellow, especially after a few malts. Downing his fifth of the evening he repaired to his co-lodger's rooms and enquired if he had ordered their taxi, for the Historian prided himself on being a punctual fellow.

His co-lodger, the Heckler, nodded in acquiescence and stubbed out the remains of the grass joint he had been enjoying. Although these men shared salubrious lodgings in a bachelor environment, there was certainly no suggestion of that going on (unlike the tardy accusations and insinuations that have dogged Holmes and Watson in recent years). The Heckler's business was Scottish history too, and in his own way he was capable of equalling the Historian in terms of fanaticism, although his wardrobe was far more contemporary and included colour. An amiable cove, he was compelled to indulge his liking for all things green on his own, for his fellow lodger was disinclined to smoke anything stronger than tobacco. Nevertheless, they were accomplices, and so they too exited briskly and full of anticipation for the evening ahead.

Simultaneously, Mademoiselle was making her own preparations in the heart of Roman Cramond, a former village steeped in its own history. Although she loved all things French with a passion, this did not detract from her fierce loyalty to the city of her birth and her commitment to the cause. The days of the Edinburgh gentleman's club were long gone. Only the old farts, the Freemasons, and the rugger buggers clung to the belief that anything positive could come out of sexual discrimination. Mademoiselle and her female cohorts always lent a certain je ne sais quoi to the proceedings, for none of the men could be expected to behave in a reasonable manner for long if left to their own devices, the drunken gets. It was even colder down by the sea and Mademoiselle was glad that her car was conveniently parked outside. She sped into town along Cramond Road South, humming a tune by the legendary Serge Gainsbourg as the lights of Muirhouse glittered almost enchantingly across the fields.

Back in town, the Art Teacher was poncing around in his stylish Southside flat. Punctuality was never an issue as far as he was concerned, and in fact he would have been hard pressed to define exactly what the word meant. Typically the artist, he was drinking chilled Prosecco despite the cold. He dressed in an unconscious imitation of Ted Hughes, although it is unlikely that Hughes would have favoured denim as his leg wear, this touch being more in the style of Martin Amis. The tweed jacket was spot on though, as was the thinly striped shirt. He knew it too, and so had adopted this outfit as his standard uniform. He was already late but he reasoned that there was still enough time for another single-skinner and another glass of this excellent Prosecco! Only when the bottle was finally empty did he deign to slip on his Dax overcoat and venture out into the cold.

'Twas indeed a perfect night for plotting and the foul weather was going to make the choice of destination all the more desirable – cellar taverns are much like caverns on nights such as this, and one of Man's primal instincts is to head for the caves. And so, the cabal gradually wound its way across the deserted city (it was a Tuesday night) and found itself in Whighams Wine Cellars. Although this clandestine jewel of a tavern did not possess a real fire, it was a plotter's dream come true, with a number of candle-lit nooks and crannies in which to hide – not to mention the staggering selection of wines on offer. At times, if you were drunk enough, it was possible to imagine yourself in the taverns of old, where business and pleasure were conducted in equal measure. Certainly, Edinburgh has a wealth of public houses, but it is unwise to confuse quantity with quality, and the majority of these can be dismissed with a contemptuous wave of the hand. Whighams was the real deal; if you went there merely to drink then you had failed miserably to appreciate one of Edina's greatest treasures. Our cabal was well acquainted with Whighams and its members made themselves comfortable in a small room at the back of the tavern. The first glasses of strong red wine were poured, although Mademoiselle declined, as drinking and driving was clearly beneath her. The Master without Honour gazed warmly at the expectant faces around him, raised his glass, and proposed a toast.

"My dear friends! Once again into the Festival of Darkness! Confusion to our Enemies!"

The Festival of Darkness had indeed begun again, in celebration of the Long Nights. As such, it was one of the few festivals in Edinburgh that retained any vestige of dignity and integrity. This is a tale of many voices, remember, and it is now time to listen to them...

Of Molluscs And Men

Words of wisdom from 'Dr. D. Bunk'

By Andy Anderson

Found a discarded bag of winkles. After picking up its wet surface, wiped my gloves along a sandstone wall to remove any decaying mucus. Then I wondered are they still alive, so I opened the bag and they smelt just like the ocean rocks and their lids were closed. What a fate for a living being.

I wandered along the street but I couldn't get away from them. I stopped and contemplated their predicament. I had a day ticket so I could take them to the sea for no extra costs, but I couldn't make up my mind so I spun a coin for a heads or tails result rather than a trigram. It came up heads, so I took the molluscs to the ocean in a state of euphoria. Everywhere the forces of destruction prevail but here was a gesture of affirmation.

In the dimly lit tide of the rocks I returned a bag of living beings to their home. I noticed that some of their lids had become detached so perhaps a few were already dead. Like a mollusc we are a drop in the ocean and all we have to do is return to our home, the undiluted acceptance of being.

Ode To Indian Nell

By our poet in exile, 'The Poacher'

By Graham Brodie

Low down Indian Nell sat
Playing his blues for his own
Measure of pleasure.

That was that.

One day an angel came his way,
Called by his music to hear him play.

Indian Nell sat for a while.
Gazing into the angel's smile.

Taken with it.

Indian Nell invited the angel
To sit with him,
High upon his pile.

The angel did this;
Sang and danced with guile.

She then turned to Indian Nell,
Cast her heavenly spell,
Down went Indian Nell,

To Hell.

Bloomsday

A Caledonian Reprise

By Seamas Joyce

Stately, plump Buck Milligan woke up late with
a sore head and a queer feeling in his guts.
Neglecting to shave, he dressed smartly and soon
found himself heading towards the heart of the
Hibernian metropolis.

He stumbled along Grafton Street, his head
spinning, and at some point – whether 100
seconds or 100 years later, he could not be sure
– burst through the door of Davy Byrne's in
search of refreshment.

He stumbled to the bar, downed a glass of porter,
then noticed to his right an aggressive fellow
citizen in heated discussion with a charming
Semite by the name of Leopold Bloom.

Bloom was getting it tight from this drunken
rebel: "Three cheers for Israel", shouts the
Shinner.

Despite the indignity of his open trousers, Bloom
stood, and reminded his critic that Mendelssohn
was a Jew, and Karl Marx and Mercadante and
Spinoza, and of course the Saviour was a Jew and
his father was a Jew.

This unveiling of truth soured the atmosphere
further, so Milligan intervened and offered to buy
them all some lunch.

MILLIGAN: Young fella, get these gentlemen
a glass of burgundy each and a gorgonzola
sandwich.

BARMAN: Oi caan't help ye, sir, they've scoffed the lot.

Milligan turned to see a coach-load of Harvard alumni eating the traditional Joycean repast in its appropriate setting while writing witty postcards home.

This added to his confusion, and he suggested to Bloom that they leave. The two made their exit, and strolled through the city's warm June sunshine.

Milligan suggested they head into Temple Bar where they'd be sure to get a drink in peace, but things had changed. Hordes of drunken Anglo-Norman invaders were parading around in rugby tops, singing and vomiting and baring their arses.

Undeterred, our intrepid heroes beat the traffic by walking to the airport and took the first cheap flight out of there that they could. By chance, they were heading to the Caledonian capital thanks to Ryanair's generous pricing. They bumped into Stephen Dedalus and were prepared for an awkward moment, but fortunately he was just back from a fortnight in Greece. Most airlines had barred him since the Icarus incident.

*

By evening, each man had sampled the pleasures that Edinburgh has to offer. Milligan had surveyed the cultural delights, the architecture, the people, while Bloom had taken a bus to Portobello beach and masturbated with the enthusiastic co-operation of a lame childminder.

Back in their hotel, Milligan flicked through the cable TV channels. Amid the confusion and cacophony, a pattern emerged:

Cilla Black Sings FLICK Stephen King's Carrie
FLICK MTV with Beavis and Butthead FLICK...

Cilla Black... Carrie... Beavis and...

Cilla... Carrie... Beavis

Cillla... Cari... B... dis

He'd had an Edwin Morgan moment.

*

The pair weaved unsteadily between the Scylla of
the St James Centre and the Charybdis of Lothian
Road in search of more drink and possibly even
some forthright conversation.

They found themselves in a dark cellar, where a
group consisting mainly of gentlemen was largely
in a state of mirth as they read aloud various
amusing epistles from a local journal. Milligan
heard occasional snatches:

"... riding pillion down Princes Street..."

"... move Donald Dewar's statue to Edinburgh..."

"St Giles' is not a cathedral..."

Bloom was uneasy at hearing talk of religion, but
need not have worried. The group numbered at
least one extreme Protestant who would be well
aware of the debt owed by his most democratic of
faiths to the Hebrew tradition.

Turning to the bar, Bloom ordered more burgundy
and found himself in increasingly earnest and
urgent conversation with the attractive barmaid,
a lass named Molly who had once sailed across
Europe on a Galway hooker called The Barnacle.

Conversation was interrupted suddenly as
he heard a crash. One of the raucous party
had disgraced himself by an act of violence,
attempting to assault a noted Leither in response
to some Whiggish tomfoolery. It was decided
to declare the premises a Tory-free zone, and
everyone breathed easily again.

With Molly about to call time, Bloom seized his
opportunity to proposition her and she thought
the priests will have to censor this God knows
doesn't everybody only they hide it if he wants
to kiss my bottom I'll drag open my drawers and
bulge it right in his face large as life and I would
say yes my mountain flower call the publishers yes
and his heart was going like mad and yes I said
yes I will Yes.

Everyone cheered as Molly declared there would
be a lock-in tonight.

Trieste-Zurich-Paris-Dunfermline 2004

When Jim Met John

A Festival Fantasy

By Craig Gibson

Chief Inspector Barney Crozier sighed as he
scrutinised the dishevelled form of his erstwhile
favourite sergeant with a troubled frown.
Bergerac was a dedicated young detective, but
once again, his drinking had spiralled out of
control, to the extent that his career was now on
the line. Crozier cleared his throat and spoke
slowly and firmly, although with a measure of
compassion.

"Jim, I want you to take a holiday. And that's
not a request, that's an order. Take two weeks
off and for God's sake get yourself sorted out.
Get some medical help or whatever it takes.
I don't have to remind you of the consequences if
you fail to take my advice."

Five hours later Jim Bergerac was propped up
on his elbows at the bar of the Royal Barge, with
a good skinful inside him. To his right, a white-
haired gentleman with a cigar and suntan was
deep in conversation with hostess Diamante Lil.

"I tell you Lil, Edinburgh is the place to be in the
month of August. That Festival! More shows
than you could ever hope to take in, and the
licensing laws! Twenty-four hour drinking, I kid
you not!" he chuckled.

The next morning found Jim drinking heavily in
the departure lounge of Jersey Airport, awaiting
the next flight to Edinburgh. He had informed
Crozier that he intended to visit some relatives

in the Highlands in order to recuperate. Ha!
Fat chance! This would be his last chance for
a serious bender before sorting his life out, he
reassured himself. Twenty-four hour drinking,
eh...?

Five hours later Jim was in a state of intoxicated
rapture. The old gent in the Barge had been
right. A proper city for the drinking man! The
revelry taking place in George Street finally
overwhelmed him, however, and he found
himself wanting to be desperately sick. He
lurched unsteadily from the busy thoroughfare
until he found a lane suitable for his purpose.
After vomiting copiously, he wiped his mouth
and surrendered to the need for a quick pint to
replace the fluid he had deposited all over the
cobbles. Looking around, he spotted a curious
little pub entitled the Oxford, and as his need
was urgent he entered without a moment's
hesitation. The pub's Spartan interior was far
removed from the gay clamour of George Street.
There was only one other guy drinking solemnly
at the bar, about the same age as himself, and
even in his inebriated state Jim could smell
cop. He ordered a beer and turned to greet the
solitary drinker.

"DS Jim Bergerac. Bureau des Etrangers,"
he slurred, proffering his hand. The stranger
grasped it warmly, with, rather surprisingly, no
hint of freemasonry. He revealed his name was
John, and that he too was a detective sergeant in
the Lothian and Borders Constabulary.

The two cops then engaged in the kind of
nauseating bonhomie that always abounds when
lawmen meet for the first time. However, once
all the shop talk was out the way John proposed
to Jim that he show him the real Edinburgh, for
this was a city where dualism was embedded

in the very foundations. This real Edinburgh
naturally involved ogling tarts in strip bars,
drinking vast quantities of alcohol in pubs of no
cultural merit, and eating revolting fried food
to be regurgitated later. As they staggered from
hole to hole, the Festival carried on around them,
regardless.

At four in the morning, in Fingers Piano Bar,
Jim thought he'd died and gone to heaven.
John assured him the best was yet to come: the
Penny Black at five. This dive was the preserve
of serious Edinburgh drinkers at any time of
the year, he stated, so just ignore all the Festival
poofters hogging the bar. The two detectives
spent the rest of the morning toasting their
new-found friendship, before staggering their
separate ways.

Although Jim and John vowed to meet up again
for another marathon drinking session, alas it
was not to be. Throughout the following years,
they battled heroically with the demon drink, but
as this has been documented elsewhere, it does
not merit a mention on these pages.

Ode To All The Orange Ladies I Have Loved

By 'The Heckler'

The only women I have ever loved
Have been Worthy Mistresses and white-gloved.
O beautiful Orange Ladies
What is Gallic Marianne next to you?
A wanton strumpet not fit to wash your feet
(Well-heeled, in a sturdy Sunday shoe).
Williamina, Phyllis, Irene, Roberta,
Matronly defenders of Britannic majesty,
Pastel-coloured guard-dogs of Protestant liberty,
Of course I never meant to hurt you.
I just failed to understand
That what you needed was a
Real
Orange
Man.

Stone Rogues

By 'The Heckler'

Ruddy faced devotees of Bacchus, night-prowlers and hapless shift-workers traversing the New Town for the solace of the Penny Black simply ignore the murmurings above them, or else attribute such whispering to the mechanics of the City at night, sustaining and refreshing itself before the dawn. Yet above the activities of men, the statues stir. These apparently silent rulers of Edina's Memory prosecute their two-hundred-year-old campaign under the standard of "Things as they Are". Towering over them all stands one, whose body is spared the indignity of being a canvas for graffitists, even of the scrutiny of curious citizens. This is Henry Dundas, King Harry IX of Scotland, legal Brahmin, Hammer of the Radicals and willing channel of English and Indian gold. And on the pedestal, these words appear: 'All the junkies fuck off'. A more gifted artist would have sensed in Dundas an Ozymandian quality, and inscribed 'Look on my works, ye Mighty, and despair!'

From this lofty vantage, King Harry's first recourse is to his commander on the ground, old Nosey, the Duke of Wellington, vanquisher both of Bonaparte and the liberties of Europe. Night after night, Dundas addresses this Tory Premier:

"How stands it, your Grace, with the Southside blackguards and the unwashed artificers of Leith?"

"Fear not, my vigorous mount and I remain ever ready to ride up the Bridge or down the Walk and, if necessary, up to the bridles in the blood of the People. You and I, Scotch and

Irish, both born in stables but of a nobler breed, have the East in our grip. How stands George Guelph, the guardian of Hanover Street, his royal patrimony?"

"It waxes hotter for him," replies King Harry. He stands too low, lacking the loftiness royalty needs as its shield. The rabble can see his fulsome proportions, and some ask why this corpulent German voluptuary should be accorded so prominent a place. One of the Nobility recently mocked his ever memorable visit to his northern province in 1822."

"Alas, it is so," interjects Sir Walter Scott, sitting thoughtfully in his Gothic throne. "I did all I could that year to attach the people to his line. He wobbled around, draped in tartan, surrounded by dragoons, fictitious clans and a loyal mass of our goodly Scotch lairds. I made a Highlander of him! Even then, some mocked, and over my glorious panegyric, Carle, Now The King Comes was posted a vulgar lampoon:

Sawney, now the King's come,
Sawney, now the King's come,
Kneel and kiss his royal bum,
Sawney, now the King's come,
In Holy-Rood House lodge him snug,
And blarnify his royal lug,
With stuff wad gar a Franchman ugg.
Sawney, now the King's come.

Tell him he is great an' gude,
An' come o' Scottish royal bluid,
Down like Paddy, lick his fud,
Sawney, now the King's come,
An when he rides 'Auld Nukie' through,
To bless you wi' a kingly view,
Let him smell your 'Gardyloo',
Sawney, now the King's come!"

The reply to Scott's lament comes from Frederick Street, from Billy Pitt, another Tory Premier and the architect of British wars against liberty: "But yet it has worked, Sir Walter. Queen Vicky drapes herself unmolested at the foot of the Mound, captivating and dazzling the poor Scotch with a misty-eyed stare to the North. Her consort and spawn have held her western position at Charlotte Square unchallenged for a century. All is well, the trick has worked and indeed, it is rumoured another Teutonic matriarch of our Royal line may be reinforcing us in the Gardens soon!"

"And Billy, my old patron and friend," whispers Dundas over the roof of Jenners, "what do our spies say of the outlying areas, the Old Town and the South?"

"Earl Haig keeps watch on old Bruce and Wallace at the Castle, while the Duke of Buccleuch – and even a mounted King Charles Stuart – are suffered to keep the peace at St Giles and the Royal Mile. In the City Chambers, the mighty Alexander and his horse, Bucephalus, remind the Magistracy of its duty and the people of their fate – the one's authority must always conquer the other's spirit."

"And Knox," adds Thomas Chalmers, founder of the 'Free' Church of Scotland and spokesman of the black-slugs of the Priestocracy, thunders only at the walls of New College and St Giles, safely out of sight and mind, disturbing only theologists and these new Lords of the Articles, who administer the country's affairs for their London masters. However, my Lord, Infidelity stalks the land unchallenged. My great fear is that its handmaidens, Democracy and Anarchy, faithfully attend it – what news of the radicals?"

"Radicals," chuckles King Harry. "Revolutionists?

My dear Dr. Chalmers, when bellies are full what
need has the rabble of Politics? Besides, Billy
and I – with the help of our loyal Scotch judges,
crushed the Jacobins – their Tricolours, Ça Ira
and Rights of Man – in 1794. All that remains of
them is a sombre and grey obelisk, voiceless and
still on the Calton Hill, locked into contemplation
of the Heavens, and the world beyond this.

"At ease, Gentleman, the dawn beckons and so
our toil comes to an end for another night. Stand
fast, however, and keep your gaze on the People.
For the moment though, all is well, and seems
still."

And with that King Harry composes himself,
resumes his 'sneer of cold command' and he
and the other Guardians of Oligarchy settle into
another day of watching over the multitudes of
the good town of Edinburgh.

Such, friends, is the state of our watchful public
monuments, forming, almost exclusively, a vile
pageant to aristocracy, priestcraft and kingcraft.
And so, the next time you see a heap erected to
a land-pirate like Buccleuch, any of our German
Royalty and particularly the elevated and
avaricious Dundas himself, don't pass quietly by
with eyes downcast – that's just what they want.
Instead, stop and raise your head to give them
a searching and defiant stare. If nothing else, it
makes them jumpy.

Situations Vacant

Edinburgh desperately requires a Leader of the
Mob, a position last held by 'General' Joseph
Smith (? - 1780). The ideal applicant will be
boisterous, energetic, unruly, and have a wealth
of relevant experience in the ancient art of
rabble-rousing. Duties will include storming the
barriers at Hogmanay, disrupting the Tattoo, and
harrassing the Council and the Lady Provost. An
ability to bang the drum loudly is desirable but
not essential as full training will be given. Please
apply by electronic mail enclosing a current CV
to: paxedina@yahoo.co.uk

'General' Joe Smith laying down the law
to the Magistrates

For The Love Of God

The Truth About Scotland's Protestant Martyr Heroes

By Robin Ruisseaux

Calvinism, it's Scotland's black experiment.
It's Holy Willies, Wee Frees, the Boys' Brigade
and, of course, brooding John Knox. With
its trumpet-blasting Books of Discipline and
ceaseless catechisms, it's just too biblical, just
too much like hard work – definitely not for the
Brodie Set.

We'd rather have the romance of Jacobite
Highlanders than the rigour of Knox and his
bleak followers, who the Anglophile historian
Lord Dacre called 'a gallery of intolerant bigots,
narrow-minded martinets, timid, conservative
defenders of repellent dogmas, instant assailants
of every new or liberal idea, inquisitors and
witch-burners!' Lowlanders: he refers to our
abject ancestors!

Where now the Orange Lodge offer vinegar, once
we had fine wine. In the seventeenth century
biblical madmen – Seekers, Ranters, Levellers,
Fifth Monarchists and, in Scotland, Covenanters
– turned the world upside down for the one and
only time in British history.

For Scots Presbyterians, the Bible, the book of
all understanding, was the dictator of Time's
narrative:

*The Lord maketh the earth waste, and turneth
it upside down... And it shall be, as with the
people, so with the priest; as with the servant,*

*so with his master; as with the maid, so with
her mistress... The earth shall reel to and fro
like a drunkard and shall be removed like a
cottage.* [Isaiah 24.1, 2, 20]

In the remarkable events of the Reformation
they saw the signs of the imminent Apocalypse,
the arrival of King Jesus, and the overthrow of
the Antichrist (generally identified as the Pope of
Rome). According to John Napier of Merchiston
– he of university fame – Scotland was marked
out for a special role in battle against the
Antichrist, and he invented logarithms to
calculate the Apocalypse's precise date as 1688.
For our forebears, bigotry equalled science and
easily translated into politics.

Charles I, Britain's Protestant emperor, wanted
to curb their wilder spiritual enthusiasms
by introducing the English practices such as
kneeling in Kirk and diktat of what could be
spoken in prayer. With typical arrogance, he
refused to seek sanction from Scots of any rank
for his innovations and demanded acquiescence.

*They have set up Kings but not by me, they have
made Princes and I knew it not.* [Hosea 8.4]

For Presbyterians such abominations smacked
of Popery and a perversion of their Reformation.
They set out to wreck the cottage of kings. In
Edinburgh, the Presbyterian mullahs provoked
an Iranian-style revolution against Charles.
Nobles, ministers and thousands of folk signed
the National Covenant of 1638 in Greyfriars
Kirkyard. Inspired by the Jews' Old Testament
covenant with Jehovah, it was a kind of marriage
contract that bound all Scots to God in pursuit of
a Scottish Parliament and a Presbyterian Kirk
free from royal control. The Covenant was for
keeps. There was no going back to God and

asking for a divorce. Terms and conditions applied in the new Israel.

It was the product of Archibald Johnston of Wariston, one of Edinburgh's most formidable legal intellects, who sifted the ephemera of his everyday experience in a vast spiritual diary – which he jotted down even on horseback or singing psalms in Kirk. In it he recorded everything from his twelve-point plan for godly governance to Scotland's first masturbator monologue. In Wariston's world, God blessed his lust for his wife and the Devil moved in the demise of a cat.

Wariston advocated Law Work, a grim form of mind-bending designed to discipline oneself to think only good thoughts. For his son, young Archie, recurring black teenage thoughts proved overwhelming and he gave himself over to Satan, an act of witchcraft punishable by burning at the stake. He took to eating dust like the sinners in the Book of Micah, before Wariston and a host of praying ministers finally dissuaded him.

For the Covenanters, the revolution wasn't fought simply by the pen and the sword. According to their spiritual leader, Samuel Rutherford, it was an experience akin to making love: 'To write how sweet the honeycomb is, is not so lovely as to eat and suck the honeycomb. One night's rest in a bed of love with Christ will say more than heart can think, or tongue can utter.'

Under Rutherford's guidance the Covenanters became more radical. Nobles were forced onto the repentance stool in Kirk; royalists purged from public life; witches hunted; unruly youths executed; fornicators, drunkards and singers of bawdy songs fined. Now that's what I call good discipline: Jesus and No Quarter – really tight.

45

You might think Rutherford's political thought is irrelevant, but you would be wrong. Today his writings are revered by American Christian fundamentalists like the anti-abortionist Operation Rescue, who aim to found a Christian Republic along Rutherfordian lines. No kidding.

But they also lie behind our own democratic traditions. In Lex Rex – 'the law of kings' – of 1644, Rutherford justified the regicide of tyrants who broke their contract with the people, from which our notions of contractual governance and the right actively to resist tyranny are derived. Protestant fanaticism lies at the very root of our rights. Think on that next time you ponder Bin Laden and his ilk.

The Covenanters' rule ended with Oliver Cromwell's invasion of 1650. The Scots commander, David Leslie, had strongly fortified the burgh walls of Edinburgh and Leith, and connected the two by an imposing forty-gun rampart – which was later levelled to make Leith Walk. His preparations were a success. After pointlessly bombarding the Capital from Arthur's Seat, Cromwell was forced to retreat to Dunbar. The Scots ministers, now confident in the Lord's blessing, pressed Leslie to attack 'like going down against the Philistines at Gilgal'. God, however, turned out to be thoroughly English – 14,000 were captured or fell on the field, Scotland was conquered and the Covenant vanquished. One can draw one's own metaphysical conclusions.

In 1660, Charles II was restored to power. One Royalist, Sir Thomas Urquhart of Cromarty, is said to have died laughing when he heard the news, but for the Covenanters the Royalists' retribution wasn't quite so amusing.

On the north side of St Giles lies the tomb of
the wily cross-eyed leader of the Covenanters,
Archibald Campbell, the Marquis of Argyll, who
was beheaded at the Mercat Cross by the Maiden
– the Scottish guillotine – and his head stuck on
a spike. Wariston followed soon after. To dare
was their politics, terror their piety.

That was supposed to be the end of it, but Argyll
and Wariston became martyrs for the cause.
The lower sort, intoxicated by the ideals of the
Covenant, wouldn't let it go and rebelled under
its banner twice in the following decades. In
the entrepôt of Rotterdam, exiles like Robert
MacWard plotted the royal Antichrist's downfall.
His pamphlets, smuggled into Edinburgh, fired
the imagination of two radical students, James
Renwick and Alexander Shields, who were
members of a secret network called the United
Societies.

In 1683, on a Lanarkshire muir, Renwick lifted
the Covenant's fallen standard and embarked on
a jihad that declared war on the state and all its
agents. On the king's birthday in 1685 he and
his followers, in an act of suicidal bravura, swept
into the burgh of Sanquhar, sang psalms and
renounced James VII as their king.

In response, the government embarked on the
persecution known as the Killing Times.

Specialist troops of rough riders pursued
Renwick and shot anyone who refused to abjure
out-of-hand his war against the state. Renwick,
the Osama of the Scots, only survived by hiding
among the remote country folk of Lanarkshire.

Taking their cue from the Book of Revelations,
the Society people saw their persecution as
analogous to that of the early Christian martyrs:

And they overcame him by the blood of the Lamb, and by the word of their Testimony, and loved not their Lives unto the Death. [Revelations 12.11]

After his capture, Alexander Shields tried his damnedest to gain a martyr's crown, but it was denied him and he was sent to Scotland's Camp X-Ray on the formidable island fortress of the Bass Rock. For two years Shields sat in his dank cell before he escaped dressed as a woman – of course – to Rotterdam. There he published his political masterpiece, A Hind Let Loose, which, in its advocacy of a democratic form of a republic, spoke like an axe.

Another prisoner of the Bass was the charismatic hellfire preacher Alexander 'Prophet' Peden. The Kendo Nagasaki of his day, Peden preached in a disguise mask that made him look like a plague victim. Armed and on the run, he preached at subversive open-air meetings on the high moors until he was apprehended and sent to the Bass. There he languished for four years, no doubt making the guards' lives insufferable by raving on about their eternal damnation, until, in 1678, when the authorities decided the Bass wasn't far enough away for Peden and sold him into slavery in Virginia. Realising that wee pale Scottish guys wouldn't last long under the lash and blazing sun of the tobacco plantations, Peden jumped ship and returned to preaching. In 1686, after twenty-two years on the run, he died and was buried at Auchinleck in Ayrshire, but not for long. The troopers who hunted him had other ideas. They dug up his corpse and hung it on the gallows. Justice must be done.

Renwick too was finally cornered in a house near Edinburgh Castle. After a brief shoot-out, he escaped down Castle Wynd to the head of the Cowgate, where, having lost his hat, he was recognised by a passer-by, tripped and captured. He refused to repent and welcomed martyrdom as he was turned over to be hanged. Like the French Revolutionary, Saint-Just, he despised the very dust from which he was formed.

Within months Napier's long-predicted Apocalypse arrived. King James was overthrown, not by the expected King Jesus, but by King Billy – Wilhelm van Oranj – armed with a blessing from the Pope. No wonder they were grateful, if a little confused by the ways of the Lord.

So next time you wander by Greyfriars, where Wariston and Renwick lie, think kindly on your Calvinists. They were no reactionary forelock-tugging Unionists intent on defending the British flag or a Protestant queen; they were ambitious for Scotland and for a world of justice.

New Puritans, it's time to love our old Calvinists, not for their bigotry or cant moralism – let's leave that to the Christians – but for their strangeness, discipline and revolutionary fervour. The time for irony is over. Let us suck on the honeycomb of our worthy ancestors and build Jerusalem anew right here in fair Edina.

Susan Boyd

A Brief Life

Alasdair Gray

Susan Boyd, television playwright, was born in
1949 and died of a brain haemorrhage on
18 June [2004] in Glasgow's Southern General
Hospital. Her mother was actress Katy
Gardiner; her father playwright Eddie Boyd, who
left his family too early to be an influence: Susan
only met and became friendly with him in her
mid-twenties.

She lived at first with her mother and
grandmother in Riddrie, one of the earliest
and pleasantest of Glasgow's municipal
housing schemes, and in a Loch Lomond-side
holiday cottage near Rowardennan. Granny, a
schoolteacher, had been wife of the archaeologist
Harrison Maxwell. Susan's home was well
furnished with books and radical ideas, artistic
and political. When Granny died, mother and
daughter moved to an equally well-furnished
flat in Great George Street, Hillhead, from which
Susan attended Hillhead Secondary School then
Glasgow School of Art. She left the last after two
years, having made life-long friends but now
sure she wished to be a writer.

Like many with uncommon ambitions she went
to London, partly to show independence from
her tolerant and strong-minded mother, and
partly because London in the 1960s seemed far
more exciting than Glasgow. It dominated the
British publishing and entertainment industries
by which she hoped to live. Several friends,
documentary filmmaker John Samson and his
wife Linda among them, were there for the same

reason. But first Susan lived for ten years on low earnings from work in factory, warehouse and street market – being a postman, a supply teacher and (for several evenings) a life model at a Civil Service art class in the War Office basement. Her mother's influence once got her employed by BBC television's wardrobe department. Pay was good, hours few, bosses and colleagues pleasant, but the job involved typing long lists of properties that stupefied the imagination she needed to write. Until able to write full-time, she preferred a variety of less middle-class jobs. These eventually equipped her to write plays with London settings.

Like many authors, her first efforts were a semi-autobiographical novel, never finished, and short stories published in short-lived literary magazines. Her first success was Another Day, a BBC 2 Play of the Week, which attracted attention by showing love between a white woman and black man. It also showed the kind of modern life Susan could dramatise. In 1985 the EastEnders series began and she was in its writing team from then until her death. She also wrote episodes of Casualty, Paradise Club and Crown Court, several single television plays and eleven for sound radio. By 1990 she was earning enough to buy a flat in Partick, Glasgow, where a computer now let her confer as closely with colleagues as she had done in London, with a few flying visits there for script conferences.

Susan liked her work and brought to it (as all who work well in television must) the integrity and cynicism of a good professional journalist or policeman. In recent years she had to struggle with many new EastEnders producers and directors whose bright ideas (she thought) ignored common sense and continuity of character. She lent money willingly, without

assurance of return, and also gave it. Her
manners were modest but socially she was
no coward, and kind to lonely, eccentric and
desperate folks. A London neighbour specialised
in finding homes for feral cats; Susan adopted
three, which she brought to Partick. She was
careful to keep in touch with friends. When
John Samson died she carefully located and
informed all his Scottish friends of the funeral
and flew down to it, despite being troubled by
intermittent headaches. She died two days after
returning. She is survived by a loving mother,
brother, sister, daughter, two grandchildren,
three very old domesticated feral cats and many,
many friends. Watchers of EastEnders may soon
notice, in the more long-standing characters, a
lack of convincing continuity with their younger
selves.

A Glass Of Wine

By James Wood

Coming home late after a hard day,
I'll sometimes have a drink.
One becomes two. Et cetera until my head protests
And I vow to quit. But tonight, I swear,
It's just the one. Stripping off the foil,
I do with the cork what I have to do,

Tilt the bottle and let its rope uncoil
Twisting into the glass like an ocean.
I've heard wine called life, or blood, or ink
By people who search for something deeper
In what they drink, their glasses chiming
In ceremony or celebration.

But tonight, alone, I lift this glass
By its stem to catch the scent
That rises from its crimson meniscus,
Watch the bubbles cling to the rim
Before they burst and vanish. Wine is nothing:
It doesn't work wonders, it can't invent

Fantastic realms where we all get
What we want, sunlit dreams
Of southern vineyards and dusky maidens.
I don't see some drunken God
At the heart of my glass, just
A red-black, tasty fluid. Still, wine seems

To bring us together; it sets alight
A dull dinner, makes us flirt or risk that pass.
It can ease the pains of early love
And the later pain of loss; it calms,
Soothes, relieves and comforts. Perhaps,
On reflection, I'll have another glass.

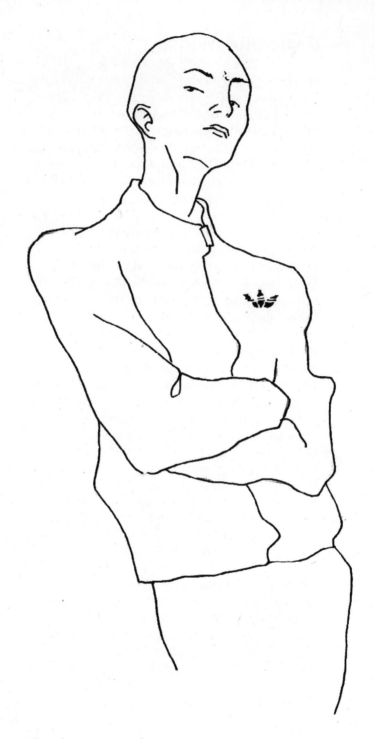

Congratulations?

Scribes of Edina! It would appear that celebrations are in order for, as we are sure you are aware, our beloved Capital has recently been awarded the title "World City of Literature". Hip, Hip Hooray! Naturally, we at the Gun are delighted that our city's great literary tradition has been recognised on a global scale, and imagine there is much dancing in the streets of Merchiston.

However, before you crack open the champagne, ponder exactly what this means for our underground army of impoverished talent. It has been noted by many observers in the media that the title will generate (yet) more money for the Capital's coffers. And how much of this newly acquired scratch will benefit tomorrow's literary heroes? Sweet Fanny Adams! No, our circumstances remain the same; we are still at the mercy of the Scottish Arts Council, an organisation that keeps the spirit of Harry Dundas alive in the new millennium.

We hope the powers that be will live up to their new responsibility. To merit fully the title of "World City of Literature", it is not enough to celebrate our established literary icons of past and present. More funding MUST be made available for dreamers and visionaries, otherwise our new title is nothing more than a "Toom Tabard". It is shameful that the only citizens who will benefit financially from our new-found glory are the usual publicans, hoteliers and peddlers of tat on the Royal Mile.

Nevertheless, keep the faith and above all, keep scribbling. If the bastards won't help us, we will have to help ourselves. The future is in our hands and we too have a responsibility.

Pax Edina!

Advice From An Uncle On Starting A Business

By Michael Conway

Get an accountant.
Failing that,
A sister.

Avoid lawyers,
Or state aid.

Frighten a bank manager
With shiny shoes,
And his competitors.

Do not borrow from him or her,
But from your Family.

Loss lead
Does not
Lead to
Loss.

The best advertising is
Word of mouth;
It is also the cheapest.

Use the best quality stationery.

Make sure you're in sole charge.

Take receipts for everything
And note every penny spent,
Even if you look like a miser,
Or seem like a prat.

Always watch out for HMIR.

Be mean with yourself,
And generous to others.

Drink in public water,
In private wine.

Tap your friends,
And pay them back copiously.

Remember:
There's nothing wrong in going bust.

Send Him A Strong Body With A Big Head And A Smart Arse To Put His Clever Working Class Self Defined Identity In

Another contribution from 'The Poacher'

By Graham Brodie

Send him a strong body with a big head and a
smart arse to put his clever working class self
defined identity in

The man feels no one is listening
His words are very important
And they are history
They must be interpreted the
Right way

The man remembers physical
Hard work
And is associated with it by
Ancestry

He yearns for a romantic past
As the present challenges
Appearing hard and wrong
Raising a need for things

In their place is where he understands

Forgetting the ebb and flow all around
His hell bent blind determination
To keep things the way they should be

Maybe
He
Will

Go dancing with the mongrels
Of which he is one
Having cocked his leg
And pissed on the past.

Time Gentlemen Please

By Jim Ritchie

Standing by the bar of the Ensign Ewart,
the soldier noticed an old man checking his
pocket watch. The old man was James Ritchie,
watchmaker of the Grassmarket, Edinburgh.
Each day as the soldier passed through the
Grassmarket on his way up to the castle he
stopped outside this watchmaker's shop.
There, he adjusted his watch to the time on the
grandfather clock in the window. It was well
known that this was the most accurate clock in
the City of Edinburgh.

Next day, walking briskly through the Old Town,
the soldier smiled as he recalled the previous
evening. Pausing outside the watchmaker's he
was more diligent than normal in checking the
time. One o' clock approached as he hurried
to climb the long steps from the Grassmarket
to the Castle. It was his duty to fire the famous
Gun on the stroke of one o' clock. He counted
the seconds as he waited to fire it. Below in the
Grassmarket the old man too waited patiently.
As the walls echoed to the sound of the gun the
old man skillfully adjusted the grandfather clock
in the window. It was well known that the One
O' Clock Gun was the most accurate source of
time in the City of Edinburgh.

Letters From A Lost Empire

Introduced by Will Lawson

When I unwrapped Grandfather's last package
in the attic, I found inside the sweet-smelling
vellum a hidden self. His life had always been
a mystery. Nothing had ever happened in
his life, he insisted. Yet, as he sat nodding by
the fireside, sola topi hanging by the assegai
he always carried, I had often wondered.
These letters, from a lost empire to my lost
grandmother, reveal distant echoes from our
glorious past.

My Dearest Emily,

The hospitality of these simple jungle folk is
often overwhelming. I recall particularly one
village where the scant population rose on my
arrival. I was seated in the centre of the village
on the only chair – indeed it was little more than
a rude stool – and surrounded by the broadly
smiling blackamoors.

After some little time and no small consultation,
one of their number produced a bowl of thin,
foully acid broth. Mindful of the need to avoid
offence, I consumed this potation with every sign
of relish.

A further bowl was put before me. This appeared
to contain little but particles of the common
beetle, indifferently macerated into a coarse
paste. This too I ate, much to the joy of the
audience. They shouted and whooped, throwing
small shells amongst themselves.

The meat course (if that is the appropriate
term) was a small jungle monkey, barely more

than raw. I gagged on this but managed, in due course, to do it some justice. At this many of the tribe commenced clapping and singing.

"Another another: he will eat another!" they called.

"No, no, by God it is impossible!" another heathen faction carolled.

A fourth bowl, at least warm this time, was accordingly placed in front of me. I had consumed only a few mouthfuls before I realised that these degraded savages had sunk so low as to consume the excrement of their domestic animals. With disgust I pushed this noisome dish from me.

The natives stood in silence and a further exchange of small shells took place amongst them. This far from the coast such objects function as primitive coinage.

Although I felt vilely nauseated as I left, I flatter myself that I brought some joy to the life of the village. Their happy laughter followed me as I continued on my quest.

Devotedly yours,
Monty.

The Young Windsors

By Keith Farquhar, aka 'The Art Teacher'

The beauty of the Windsors
When they were young
Elizabeth Margaret Anne
A famous photograph of Anne
Breasts caught on the upward gallop
Whilst riding a horse
By Lichfield or someone.

The Dashing Mr Digges

An appreciation by 'The Doctor'

By Cathy Scrutton

One may occasionally wonder if the Gun gazes
backward too lovingly upon the glorious heyday
of the Athens of the North. Well, I challenge
those of you of such commendably modern
mindset to produce from today's green rooms
and theatre bars a character as charming, as
hip and as handsome (and accompanied by
that same attractive frisson of illegality) as was
Mr West Digges, a paragon of the eighteenth-
century Edinburgh stage. Which member of the
Hallion Club, which Traverse stalwart can match
this stylish blade's reputation and devastating
stage presence? Is there anyone treading
Edinburgh's boards in the new millennium who,
as Mr Boswell asked, 'has more or as much of the
deportment of a man of fashion?' For the diarist
could think of none; and Mr Digges' audience,
ladies and gentlemen alike, was similarly
captivated – and scandalised.

Not a little scandal rubbed off on anyone daring
to profess themselves actor or actress in the
1750s. The thespian found himself in a position
perhaps resembling that of today's cannabis
smoker; whilst enormously popular, all dramatic
entertainment not licensed by Royal Patent and
an Act of the British parliament – and there
seemed fat chance of that – was prohibited.
To get around this, the theatre was cunningly
named the Canongate Concert Hall.

The acme of Mr West Digges' celebrated
career was perhaps his staging there in 1756 of
Douglas, an ecstatically-received tragedy penned

– shockingly – by a Church of Scotland minister (soon to become an ex-minister for his pains). Digges, naturally, graced the stage as leading man. The Caledonian Mercury doubted that any could improve upon his performance. The Kirk, however, soon out-dramatised the show with its outraged censure of ministers who attended and its fierce Admonition condemning the Luxury, Levity and Licentiousness of the Age. There was even an attempt to jail the Star himself for debt, an occupational hazard for a dandy which had afflicted Digges since his army days. Luckily for his admiring public, he escaped, the Kirk's blustering backfired and the affair hastened the decriminalisation of the theatre.

The son, it was said, of an earl, despite his pecuniary position, the dashing Mr Digges' fine breeding, elegant bearing and bona drag complimented those rakish good looks. Whenever The Beggars' Opera, a notorious satire of the day, played in the Canongate, he shone in the role of Captain Macheath, the highwayman anti-hero with two strings to his bow. Off-stage, the actor-manager's allure was equally potent; by all accounts, including at least one from an angry husband, he was a well-known Lothario whose libertinage was widely indulged. Boswell thought Digges a swell, recording his youthful idolisation in his Journals and carefully modelling himself on our voguish man about town.

Digges filled the gossip columns with talk of his passionate flings with his leading – and often married – ladies. Soon after his Edinburgh debut, he seduced the actress Mrs Sarah Ward, who had founded the Canongate theatre. Digges' fiery affair with his professional and private Juliet smouldered, albeit with the odd flame of friction, for several years. When the curtain finally came down upon their torrid liaison, it was not long before Digges reappeared with his arm around the glamorous and equally debt-ridden Mrs George Anne Bellamy. Recently escaped from creditors south of the border, elaborately clothed and bejewelled, the feisty prima donna had wowed the Westland Shires by debuting despite the partial destruction of the stage and her costumes by rioting fanatics. Digges is said to have been devoted.

Indeed, riots religious and political decorated Digges' career. Theatres were apparently destroyed and rebuilt with regularity. In 1753, a mob of zealots more suited to the Historian's chronicles tore down a playhouse in the Westland Shires where Mr Digges and Mrs Ward were appearing. Unruffled, our protagonist pursued his paramour to Ireland, where he shortly became embroiled in a political scandal. In Dublin, Digges was banned from encoring with a speech which appeared to reflect allegorically on ever-delicate Anglo-Irish relations. Displeased by the censorship, Whigs incited a riot which demolished the house and compelled the manager to flee. Back in Edinburgh, sedan chair carriers (who were hitherto allowed into the theatre gallery) violently objected to the portrayal of the working class in a performance entitled High Life Below Stairs and attempted to dismantle the Canongate stage. By the time the oft-repaired playhouse was finally razed by the mob, however, Digges had been obliged to leave town, once again in the shadow of debt.

Some years later, Mr Digges returned – where from is a Heathcliffian mystery – to become lessee of the exciting new Theatre Royal in Shakespere's Square at the east end of Princes Street. Digges was as charismatic and as

popular as ever as ladies' man Macheath, his
tour de force gaining him a new devotee in a
respectable young man named William, later
Deacon, Brodie. The Deacon is said to have been
inspired to future felony by Macheath and his
gang of seditious ne'er-do-wells populating The
Beggars' Opera; and so Mr Digges can perhaps
take his place among the originators of the
dualistic tradition which has infected the streets
of Edinburgh ever since.

What Mr Digges continued to win in acclaim,
however, he continued to lose from his wallet,
and the recurrent spectre of debt was eventually
to chase him from the Edinburgh stage.
Extricating himself once more from debtors'
gaol, the Capital's favourite philanderer took the
road to London, where he was to become known
for his Shakespearean anti-heroes. Of course,
he was not without his favourite companion for
such a journey – somebody else's wife.

Situations Vacant

The One O'Clock Gun desperately requires a
suitable arena for the purpose of winter plotting,
as Whighams has treacherously succumbed to
the worship of Mammon. Yes, the interior of this
hallowed institution, which began life as Earl
Haig's wine cellar, now resembles a pale copy
of the Opal Lounge, or any of those ten-a-penny
so-called 'style' bars disgracing George Street
with their beshitted and unwelcome presence.
Any city centre tavern where convivialia
is encouraged will be considered, and the
successful applicant will be amply rewarded with
a place in the pantheon of public houses beloved
of the Gun. Come, join us in making history!

Lateness

A Festival Reverie For Mr J^{as} C____

By Michael Conway

How many times a blow
Comes
from a no
Show?
A minute or an hour,
Say titter to a pedant;
But three or four seconds
Means aeons to a
... bore.

Ages I waited, and time I spent
Waiting for him to frequent
The place we had arranged.

The bar was full, busy and bad,
People there were,
Crazy and mad;
And still he came not,
Was I so bad?
Never, or not?
Or...

Look you. The clock. Is ticking.
Dickory, dickory, dock...
Phones they are buzzing
From home and afar
Here is the friend;
Others bizarre.
Yet, imagine the joy,
If you entered that
Door.
You on the stairs
Me on the floor!
But here in the slosh

As you rake in the
Dosh
I suddenly feel
Arteries
Thickening.

Consider another. M. Sylvain.
French-useless.
A wondrous span
Useless, though,
Because he's late
Always, late.

Amuse yourself, wrist
Watch.
Wanker's daughter
On left arm;
Born before wedlock
Begun!
Sing, little noise
Saying...
No-one, no-one.

All around me are those I fear.
Dreadful folk full of beer.
Where are you?
Friend so dear,
In another's hands?

Beneath me are sodden planks
Before me are dreadful banques
Yet I see;
No little thanks
For praising you so near?

Here I am, sitting still
Avoiding far both health and hill
Thinking of you still
Yet you're not here
Nor ever will.

Begone rapscallions of my mind
And time take you.
For James will turn up sometime
(or fate – make you).

The Bastard King And The Birth Of The Glorious Republic

By Paul Carter

I am fortunate enough to have met Marcus, the Bastard King, and indeed, long ago, spent many an evening in his company at the gentlemen's club that dare not speak its name. The club has long been nothing more than a fond memory of a select few enlightened citizens of our fair Capital, but in those days the cultural well-being of the city was moulded and refined by its members, and many a momentous event took place behind the veil of secrecy which adorned its boundaries. Of all of these events, the crowning and subsequent abdication of the Bastard King and the birth of the Glorious Republic of Edina recurs to me most often in my reminiscences, and I here commit the story to print for the first time.

Being then a great friend of the Art Teacher, the Poacher and the Master without Honour, Marcus the Bastard had developed an ailment due to excesses that led him to seek advice from a doctor of repute at the Potterow. Among the many cures and courses advised by the good doctor was the suggestion that Marcus acquaint himself with the hitherto unknown quality of his lineage, as a knowledge of such a thing might inform him as to his propensity to the follies of excess. Residing less than a mile from Register House and less than a Scots mile from the Church of Scotland House for the Resettlement of Protestant Bairns on George Street, such knowledge was easily gained by Marcus. To his astonishment, the account of his earliest day on God's earth mentioned only that he had been discovered in a shoebox on the esplanade of Edinburgh Castle.

Whether Marcus was a bastard prince who had been placed at the door of his rightful home, or merely a pitiful urchin, became the question that occupied every enlightened mind and resonated through every discussion at the meeting of the club that night. At many a point, Marcus himself seemed detached from the proceedings, and indeed forgotten in the verbose mêlée that ensued. One member dwelt heavily on the detail that a note had been pinned to the babe and was at pains to express his surprise that – if Marcus were indeed heir to the throne – the note had been inscribed only with the word 'Protestant', and made no mention of his royal rights. Many a member took exception to this judgment, conjecturing that, in a state of hysteria, his mother may well have chosen to mention only the most important of facts regarding the babe's identity, omitting all else during the hurried act of abandonment.

Very little ground was gained by either side for most of the evening until one member, who was particularly respected for his knowledge of the legal and ethnological specifics of Scotland, questioned those defending the status quo. "What is to be lost were we to acknowledge Marcus the Bastard as our rightful King?" he asked. "The House of Windsor pays us no heed! Is this not the opportunity to have the ear of our monarch within our reach? And does a man carrying the cognomen 'the Bastard' not represent our people more aptly than a woman 'of Windsor'?"

The respected member continued thus: "My paltry knowledge of such matters leads me to believe that all we require to commit such an act of perceived treason are the signatures of twelve honourable gentlemen stating their intention to uphold the claim of the pretender. The pretender will then be thrust into the royal arena from which

he must be forcibly removed, or recognised. Are
there not exactly twelve of us beside our Bastard
King tonight? All Hail the King!" And so it was
that the declaration of the House of Greenan
was signed and copies sent to Idi Amin Dada,
Elizabeth the Second and her unfortunate Prince
of Wales. No reply was received within twenty
days, with the exception of a kind (dictated) letter
from Idi Amin Dada wishing good fortune upon
Marcus the Bastard.

Marcus was now Bastard King of our Land, but
no signature had been more difficult to extract
on that historic evening than that of Marcus the
Bastard King himself. A cloud of melancholia
seemed to hang above the new monarch's
head from that day forth, and his propensity to
indulge in life's excesses seemed exacerbated
by the weight of his new-found responsibilities.
Whether the unknowable will of God guided his
actions for the duration of his short reign, or
whether the unfathomable logic of hard liquor
had taken control of the King's mind, became
the stuff of chatter. His behaviour became
increasingly erratic and fits befell him in the
taverns, involving the speaking of strange tongues
and the chewing of carpets. Constitutional
decisions were taken during these fits that were of
great significance and perhaps would have been
best resolved in the realm of clarity visited by the
mind only in the hours between breakfast and
luncheon. The most momentous of these was the
dissolving of the kingdom, performed under a
table in the Port of Leith on the first day of Lent.
Among the finer details of the act were the gifts of
Orkney to Argentina, West Lothian to the City of
Westminster and the entire region of Strathclyde
to the State of Ulster which, in turn, had been
gifted to the peoples of West Africa. By dawn,
only the fair city of Edina remained under the
control of the Bastard King.

74

A decision of even greater gravity was to come,
a decision that made visible God's rhyme and
reason within the seemingly hysterical stream
of decrees. It is no wonder to the educated and
enlightened mind that the idea of monarchic
absolutism should sit uneasily upon the
shoulders of a man raised in an atmosphere of
Protestant egalitarian radicalism, and so it was
with the Bastard King. On Good Friday, the King
arrived at the club in great spirits holding aloft
a letter, written in his own hand, announcing
his abdication. To be honest, in my recollection,
the presentation of the letter came neither as a
surprise to the other members, nor was it met
with dismay, but rather a sense of relief. This
relief became euphoria on the presentation
of a second document outlining the King's
only condition governing his abdication: that
Edinburgh be declared the Glorious Republic of
Edina. The document contained plans for the
nurturing of a cultural revolution and a one-
thousand-year epoch of enlightenment, and
footnotes explaining the necessity of gifting West
Lothian to the City of Westminster in pursuit
of this goal. All that was missing from the
document were the very signatures that had given
the King the power that he now so dearly sought
to surrender to the people.

I see the men who deposed the House of Windsor
and ushered in the dawn of the Glorious Republic
infrequently now, which saddens me. My spirits
are warmed, however, whenever I recognise
the embryonic shoots of the Glorious Republic
of Edina springing up around this fair city and
remember their father, Marcus the Bastard King.

C21H22N2O2 And The Fun That Can Be Had

By Karl Plume

Hubrey Gharbully sits on his porch bench handling some tobacco, with a golden-brown meerschaum pipe dangling from his mouth. He looks out across the field before his house. Not another building in sight; only some dismal shrubbery and an apple tree *(Hubrey had noted apples missing from the lower limbs of his tree several weeks earlier. "That's odd," he had told Ferro Ferri, who had listened astutely before returning her tongue to her anus. Apples had continued to vanish in steady numbers. "How dreadfully fucking irritating!" Hubrey had bellowed; Ferro Ferri had responded on this occasion by stirring from a light kip and momentarily opening one eye apathetically. "Whoever is doing this is a shit of the highest order!" Severely disturbed, in more ways than one, Hubrey had proceeded to infuse the tree's remaining fruit with a strong solution of strychnine.)* stand between him and the pebbly path which leads to town. As he lights up he smiles.

The door behind Hubrey leads to a dingy kitchen. In one corner a radio emits the clicks, clacks and bangs of Fred Astaire. On one wooden chair lies Ferro Ferri, a black-and-white, and somewhat plump, cat; on another rests a green-and-white cushion. The kitchen table is bare except for a slender, blue book and a hypodermic syringe.

Hubrey enters the kitchen and places his spent pipe on the book before pouring himself a glass of brandy. He sips a little and winces as the alcohol finds an inflamed area of his gum. He passes through to the bathroom where he begins urinating. As he returns to the kitchen, he sights a boy climbing over the gate which leads to his field. He knocks back the rest of the brandy and switches the radio off. The boy, Hubrey supposes, is roughly twelve years old, though gives an impression of being slightly older. His outfit consists of dull jeans and a grey T-shirt which flaunts the word 'Innocent'. Such a small body would not be difficult to dispose of. Hubrey's breathing begins to quicken slightly as the boy approaches the apple tree. The misdeed is fairly uninteresting: three apples taken; one directly bitten into. An expression of distaste pervades the boy's face as he casts the first apple aside. He selects another and bites into it with similar effect... The effects of the toxin are illustrated promptly: the boy stumbles to his knees and begins convulsing like a strychnine victim, an epileptic or a biblical pig.

At this point Hubrey emerges from his house and advances upon the boy screeching: "That'll teach you, you thieving shit! Die! Die! Expire! Give up the ghost! Evil little shit!" The boy carries on juddering. He almost manages to get to his feet, but a quick jerk of his muscles throws his balance off again. "Die! Die! Hurry up and die!" Hubrey begins kicking the boy in the stomach and, to his delight, finds that this seems to exacerbate the symptoms. As time goes by, Hubrey begins to grow bored and decides to get another drink. He doesn't know how protracted a strychnine victim's death can be. After his frenetically sadistic outburst, he's feeling drained and so makes his way to the porch bench and sits with a peevish, little sigh. He observes the boy's continued fitting with ever dwindling interest. A current of lethargy overwhelms him. He shuts his eyes and dreams:

– the boughs of a tree drag back in blustery
weather taut like the tug of expanding spinning
– the fingers of the branches and the buds upon
them are suckered into a hypodermic needle
end held aloft by the oversized, disembodied
paw of Ferro Ferri which is a trunk – Hubrey
stands in front of this stepping backwards with
elephant legs – dwarfed by its dimension his
limbs haggard beside the tree strain to reach with
a new suppleness to embrace each onerous apple
distended with sap and flesh – legs become closer
to arms until his fingers are sinking into the core
of the fruit and his feet are back on the porch
struggling to locate a hold on a chair with four
doorknobs – Ferro Ferri – no longer corporeal his
hands sink faster and faster anticipating hitting
a woody pip – the skin splinters and ejaculates
fluids which sluice him across his hand and lead
him to a certain –

Hubrey awakens with a start. The firmament
has become somewhat murkier and Ferro Ferri
is meowing and clawing at the kitchen's screen
door. He rises and unfastens the door and the cat
bounds out.

Once Again Into The Festival Of Hope (cont'd)

The Burial Of Issue # 1

On the third Sabbath of the month of April, 2004, the remaining 100 copies of the One O'Clock Gun, issue # 1, were interred in the Scottish Borders.

18th April. The Master without Honour, Mademoiselle Wyllie, the Heckler, the Art Teacher and the Historian of Fanaticks left Edina in convoy heading south, pausing only to drop in on the convivial Laird, Mulholland of Eldinhope, at the Gordon Arms. The Borders Porsche Club were also in attendance, but were scorned by the burial party whose vehicles were decidedly French in origin. Refreshed, the party sped stealthily past Altrive towards their goal.

When the rutted track finally overcame the small cars, the party dismounted to continue on foot. The last 100 were firmly bound in survival bags and Duct tape, accompanied by a signed testimony, including the signature of the Doctor who was busy tending the young in the Westland Shires. Top hats, bowlers, flat caps and partisan headgear were donned, and digging tools were selected. On the stroke of one the party set off into the hills. Their destination? Robert Wringham's grave, the most cursed and wretched literary site in all Scotia. Their aim? To give issue # 1 a fitting send off, and to reclaim the spot as a place of beauty and celebration for future generations.

An uphill trek ensued, the party in single file. There was an abundance of merriment to accompany the wheezing and red faces, and the whisky breaks were much appreciated by all. Two hours later, after a prolonged battle with the Forestry Commission's bastard invaders, they found themselves on their chosen summit. The Reverend Doolan being unavailable on this solemn occasion, the Art Teacher nobly stepped forward into the role of Gravedigger. Donning the Mask, he conducted the funereal rites with dignity, and the party paid their last respects to their firstborn.

And what next? Well, of course, they repaired to Tibbie Shiel's, the Borders howff beloved of Hogg, Wilson and Scott. They feasted upon beef, quaffed Guinness and whisky, and engaged in sublime camaraderie with the hostess. Perfection.

Editor's note: if anyone wishes back issues of # 1, please read James Hogg's Private Memoirs And Confessions Of A Justified Sinner and dress appropriately. The burial site can be found with a little effort, and the views are stunning. Hogg's classic can be ambiguous, however, so good luck.

Above: Keith Farquhar (the Art Teacher) at the burial site as depicted in Number 2.

By Craig Gibson

Editor's Introduction:
Volume II (2005)

The second volume of the One O'Clock Gun was radically
different, in many ways, from the first. Towards the end
of 2004 relations between my two co-editors and myself
had soured to the point where we were no longer able to
work together, and so I assumed full editorial control of
the paper. This schism also resulted in the departure of the
majority of the old 'Top Slot' crew but, as they say, the show
must go on. Well, as I said in my previous introduction,
the house style was already becoming a tad passé so I didn't
shed too many tears. In fact, I was surreptitiously relieved
to find myself in a position to be able to take the paper
forward in which ever way I saw fit. I was ably assisted by
Gerry Hillman, who had come on board as our designer
from issue # 2 onwards, and internationally renowned
artist Lucy McKenzie who joined the team as our resident
illustrator.

We were determined to start afresh and so we decided to do
away with the old masthead and literally re-brand ourselves
simply as 'The Gun', though we retained the cunningly
folded broadsheet format. New writers had to be recruited
too, and in a hurry at that, but thankfully I had done a bit
of networking at Seán Bradley's excellent Thirsty Lunch
literary salons during the previous Festival and, as a result,
met many like-minded individuals who were willing to
contribute their talents to the cause. Far from being cowed
by the disruption in our ranks, we realised that we now had
the potential to be a force to be reckoned with.

Though most of our writers continued to write under
aliases, this was about the only link with our previous
incarnation. We felt it highly important for the paper to
maintain an unquestionable Edinburgh character, but at
the same time we strove to publish the best literature we
could lay our hands on, regardless of content, so long as it
entertained or provoked. This entailed that some of our
contributors were not necessarily citizens of Edina, but

the new-style Gun proved to be a hit and we were able to increase our distribution from 3000 to 4000 copies per quarter.

Volume II arguably set the precedent for the subsequent volumes; the literary house style was a thing of the past, but the visual house style was firmly established. This combination of combatative writing, beautiful illustrations and meticulous presentation was about to shoot the Gun into literary infamy.

Craig Gibson

Swim

By Graham Brodie

Thomas Elver Edison
a swimmer by God's
design

Travelled the Atlantic
from A to E
Carrying the message

Electricity

Beaching himself
belly up
tongue buzzing

Abrim with conversation

Transmitting
receiving prizes

Ideas lighting

Every castle crowning

Every rocky outcrop
bowing

Dark places lit
night now bright

Work day longer
business stronger

Hard working people
Beaten
Downed
Stilled
Unwell
on the electric circuit

Drums For Sandie Craigie

By Angus Calder

Forgive me presently absent, present Sandie
if I begin with a semi-formal sonnet.

The drums of the Coogate are muted
    the day...

The depth of dying is the mass of life
whichever way one's circumscribed
    by world.
The seaman is tossed shrouded in the sea,
the fireman's fried in town and that
    wee girl's
found murdered in the wood.
    Discriminate
we must, though. Perish in the line
    of duty
is not the same as rapist's crazed
    attack
nor the sick writer drinking towards death
hastened by costly silliness. It would
be good to meet a death appearing good,
resigned and peaceful: a flag slowly furled,
the petals of a flower gently curled
in presence of some person like a wife...
(but flowers past their use-by stink
    like old man's pee).

The drums of the Coogate debate
    your swift going...

Proceed, bear with me, to a parody
of Rabbie, who'd have loved a pal like you...

O see ye bonnie Sandie as she gangs
    doon the Coogate,
her dress all disjaskit but her verses

in order –
if black eyes could flame, she has
    them, my mate,
and her well-tuned tongue booms
    across any border...

While the drums of the Coogate are
    beating the day...

Your voice of the people confronted
    all clearances.
No landlord nor boss save death
    could defeat you.

Now the drums of the Coogate beat
    for you.

Your voice had both politeness and searingness.
I cannot believe the Grim Reaper
    could cheat you.

Coogate drums aye beat for you.

So your tongue echoes on to all distant places –
the windmill farms of County Mayo,
Caithness radioactive beaches,
the hashish gardens of far Morocco
and wherever the last Taiwan tiger may lurk...

So the drums of the Coogate climb the
    air
and the drums of the Coogate climb the
    air
and the drums of the Coogate climb the
    air.

The Iron Law Of The Country

By Michael Conway

The problem with the one-trick pony was that
even its one trick was not very good. At a given
signal, usually my whistle, the pony would raise
its right fetlock, bend it at the paten, neigh,
and urinate, all at the same time. Not what one
in the cities would call a polite performance, I
grant you, but we're country folk, and the one-
trick pony's antics made the kids scream with
delight. But they are all grown-up now, and far
away.

I had already dispatched the French poodle that
morning. Problem was it was toothless. Not
much use for ratting, I can tell you, a toothless
poodle! Of course, it was smart enough to catch
the odd mouse, in order to avoid the law of
the country. No teeth, no Chum. (Of course, I
didn't actually give it any Pedigree Chum, but
only cat food I got at McKeown's at 9p the tin.)

McKeown was on his way to collect the poodle
corpse, and he had suggested, through my wife,
that anything else I had to hand would be useful
to justify the journey. I thought about it, and
phoned him up.

"I've got this old pony. Doesn't pay its way.
Hay costs are dreadful this weather, you know.
Would it do?"

"Och aye, but di ye mind telling me how ye dealt
wi the poodle."

I was surprised.

"Twelve-bore. To the head."

"Then will ye be careful and use a .22 on the pony? And avoid the head."

"Very well, if that's what you want," I said, signing off, and putting down the phone, a bit nonplussed.

I went to the gun case, replaced my 12-bore, took out the .22, and placed some shells in my ammunition pouch, carefully locking the door, according to law.

Now for the pony.

*

I passed my wife feeding the chickens in the yard. We didn't say anything as we passed. We knew each other that well. Perhaps too well. In fact she was the one, who, as I said before, suggested the pony to McKeown.

I went to the stable. There was the pony, Sechy by name, munching away on my money. "Not any more you're not, Sechy," I thought, as I went for its halter and pulled it out of the stall.

It was pure black, with a full mane, and what horsemen call a tie round the throat, of even blacker intensity, though there was the odd spike of grey here and there. I went for my gun. None of the unpleasantness this morning, when the poodle definitely guessed its time was up, I assumed: horses of any description are much more stupid than even the dimmest dog or bitch.

I raised the gun. And then something happened. The beast began doing its trick! The leg rose, the neighing, the fountains of urination. I fired the gun. The pony was no more.

*

McKeown arrived in his red van, known all over the county, but usually smelt first.

"Good day, Mr McKeown, here they are as promised. £80, I think."

"Indeed, here ye are," said the red-faced old man, handing me an envelope. There was no need to count it.

"Tell me, Mr McKeown," I said, "Why do you pay such a good price for a pair of such carcasses? What on earth can even a knacker do with an old pony and French poodle?"

McKeown sat down on an old stump and pulled his clay pipe from his pocket. He carefully lit the contents, then said:

"That's why Ah was most careful about the method of, er, as my Belgian friend puts it, the mode d'emploi.

"Pony brains, or as my agent prefers to call it, cerveaux de petits chevaux, are in great demand. And di ye ken why? Have yi ever heard o' saveloys? Much of the population of London live on nothing else, or so Ah hear.

"But cerveaux de petits chevaux go into the most expensive saveloys o' aa, they yins served with gulls eggs and other delicacies in the maist exclusive West End gent's clubs. Or so Ah'm tellt, by ma agent ye ken."

He tapped his pipe on the ground, and relit it.

"The rest of the meat, ye ask? Well the Spanish have a type o' strang sausage. Caad a chorizo,

Ah'm tellt. Dinnae see it much o thir aroon
this wy. Would nae gan doon too weel wi the
churchy folk, Ah gether.

"But, ye ken, for the higher end o' the market,
say state dos at the Palacio Oriente in Madrid, or
the like, they prefer a wee touch o' pony in their
chorizo. Ye micht say, a wee touch o' class."

I stared at him, half-thinking of upping
my price, since the old rogue seemed to be
supplying, as they say, the crowned heads of
Europe, but a deal's a deal – yet another of the
iron laws of the country.

"And the poodle?"

"Ah'm glad ye asked me that," he said. "Ah'd
like tae get it aff my chest. Aa the dogs Ah
get, they gan intae ma cat food." He laughed.
"Kinda poetic isn't it? Cats eatin dogs. Of
coorse, we ca it rabbit-flavour stew." He
chuckled heartily.

I bristled somewhat.

"Och aye," he added gleefully, "Ah'll sell their
black pelts tae the carpet man, as weel."

I further thought of upping the price, but again
dismissed the idea. I knew his game now, and
would use it in future to my advantage.

*

With a cheery wave he was on his way, in the
red, stinking hearse. I broke my gun, ejected
the spent cartridge, and reached out for my
ammunition pouch. The wife's teeth have
definitely been deteriorating of late, I thought.

Above: 'As recommended by The Fox on the Box.' Lucy's illustration for Number 5's display cases.

Author Interview

Peter Burnett speaks to Cameron Swinnie

Edinburgh rubble, broken arches, monuments crumbling to dust, roofs open to the sky, broken words litter this world of thought and loom forebodingly against the horizon. Nobody writes about this city any more. A strange collection of men and women walk amidst the debris, some full of lamentation, calling for urgent repairs, for an immediate restoration of the old house of the intellect. Others climb on to a prominent broken pillar and in self-confident voices explain it all away. From none of this activity does humanity derive much.

The Balmoral is an old-fashioned Edinburgh hotel. The waiters, you feel sure, could offer opinions on the '45; the lounge is gentlemen's clubbish and the pictures on the walls are naturalistic, art-as-comfort oils.

Twenty-one last February, Cameron Swinnie remains one of the most highly respected authors in Scotland and England. He has come from his home in Lochee with his companion and helpmate, Penelope, to receive an honorary degree from Napier University, his seventh to date. Cameron arrives at the appointed place in the Balmoral precisely fifteen minutes after six, impeccably turned out, six foot one and in the mood for dancing.

The carefully-chosen dress for this interview is a sombre t-shirt and Slum Shoddy brand cap. Cameron must get ragingly bored with folk telling him he doesn't look his age, and it's true. He's twenty-one but you wouldn't think he was a day over forty. For small-talk, then, while the photographer conflates his zoom, I tell Cameron that he's looking good, but his mind is elsewhere.

"I have to ask," he says, "do you ken where I can get a pie?"

He's almost coy and he lifts his sunglasses to prove it. Pictures pop into my head: one of the author as teenager, his mother admiring her son as he writes his first short stories on the lawn outside. His mother seems so butch with arms folded, with her moustache and apron. In life and in his fiction, Cameron Swinnie notices the male within us all. More. You can see it in the sidelong glances when we talk about men. He likes men. At the same time it could not be said that Cameron is just one of the boys. Life in Leith, a driven sense of purpose, and the frightening literary reputation – overlong novels, worm-holed with the same descriptions of sex and drugs. Then there are the monstered critics, the bairns babooned, the curries thrown at his editor, and of course the time he called Janice Galloway a Chinkie.

Meet Swinnie in the flesh, and you are forcefully reminded of this hardness. Cameron Swinnie – and the work he produces – glory in nothing less than a granite exterior, with a concrete centre. That his settings and characters are often drawn from the solid detail of Swinnie's own life is an open business.

Some of that experience was detailed in Swinnie's autobiography, Like I Sais (2002). Other aspects of his life, such as his Presbyterian beginnings as Cameron Camberg of Peterhead, are, according to his family, total lies. Then there was his stormy relationship with Poetry Review, his years of poverty, his conversions to

and from Catholicism, and the publication of his
first novel just before his fourteenth birthday. It
stops then, he says, because "everybody knew
what I was doing after that. I was writing novels
like there was naw tomorrow."

I confess to being astonished. In Like I Sais,
the silent, objective evidence of truth seems
miles from the football stories and the club
scenes. What sort of mind sets every third scene
of a novel in a night club? A constitutional
mentalist? Someone whose sincerity has, at
some crucial time, been questioned by the likes
of Janice Galloway?

Then something clicks. "Janice does interest
me," he says, "because fiction is lies. And in
order to write these lies you have got to have a
very good sense of what is the truth. Of course,
there is a certain truth that emerges from a
novel, but you've got to know the difference
between fiction and truth before you can write
the novel at all. A lot of novelists don't and what
you get then is a mess. People run away with
the idea that what they are writing is the truth.
What was I talking about?"

He puts his gaze on full-beam. "I can't mind
what that's got tae do with Janice, though."

Swinnie's first novel, Don't Pay The Ecky Bill,
had ethnic cookery in spades. On the surface
of it, it's a book about writing a book, about a
guy who wants to write a book, and finds a way
of writing the book through his own writing.
Underneath however, it's really about the nature
of reality and truth, and about disembodied
voices, death and psychosis.

"I got the idea from Janice, funnily enough,"
says Swinnie, "but I don't know if she minds

95

that. She suffers from delusions and aural
hallucinations which suggest to her that
actually she's a robot creation of the Scotsman
newspaper. It's really not fair, because she gets
these notions and we all have to calm her down."

Of course, such madness and the crowning
epiphanies of state-sponsored moaning are
part of Scottish literary tradition, but literary
London, less well read in these matters, was
confounded when Swinnie himself landed at
King's Cross and demanded a sausage supper
with salt and sauce. Since then, the conmen
and blackmailers, the compulsive liars and the
self-dramatists, the actresses and the image-
merchants, the media darlings and, of course,
the other writers – all of them have been
demanding salt and sauce with everything from
their cornflakes to their sushi. Swinnie has stuck
to his guns, however.

"I wouldnaw even take it on a pie," he says. "It
was just one of those mad moments that caught
on, ken? It's fir sausages and fish and that's
that."

Talking about his own talent bores him. And
you'll wait a long while for Swinnie to give
experience of some things that have happened to
him.

"In Cencrastus there's a photograph of you
bottling a postman," I say, "but none of you
writing. Are you creatively very private? Does
it pour out of you when you're locked in ecstatic
union with your own mind?"

Swinnie's face lights up like a starlet's at the
mention of violence and in a contained flurry
of words, he makes an assertion of definite
pleasure doubtless related to the memory of

what his drug dealer dished out some sixty minutes ago.

"I'm now 21 and I think the happiest years started between 13 and 15," he says. "Apart from hang-overs and nae being able to afford a car till I was fifteen-and-a-half, and a few things like that, I am much happier now. For one thing, I know how to handle my drugs. Up till the time I was 18, I was never very capable of buying any good gear. Now I am."

"You're more confident?" I ask.

"Naw I'm rich," he says. "And that's the writing for you."

I can tell we're moving towards Cameron's most immediate enthusiasm – the novels and plays that he's working on.

"I'm also writing a story called Penetrating Motherwell," he says, "based on old porn photographs and Indians. Carry-outs that is."

Penelope, who has been sitting in the corner this while, comes forward to show us both the time. A drinking companion is waiting somewhere, a gang of football fans intent on early-evening methadone is probably preparing to storm Swinnie's lounge in an effort to collapse in one record-breaking heap. Cameron Swinnie is not done, though.

"When I was ten," he says, " I was so fascinated by the war in Kosovo, so much so that I neglected everything else. It's like a cheap, violent, pornographic novel. A whole colony of ethnic Albanian women can't go back because they have nae whise to go. Their houses burned down, they've got children, the men have either disappeared or been killed. They've got nothing, nothing at all, not even an education. Sometimes it makes you sick that you can't come up with this stuff, when the world is obviously full of it, ken?"

Before leaving, Swinnie enscribes a copy of his Hollywood travelogue, Pish Upon A Star (2001) in a handwriting that is barely erect. What he wishes me is luck; what the book wishes me is its leitmotif. Remember you are a star. Then he goes on his way, talking about the state of Eckydom, rejoicing, one hopes. Rejoicing in the next 60 years of red-faced moaning.

"You Stink, Sir, I Smell"

By Robin Vandome

Bugger this sodden provincial pseudopolis; here
we all are, waiting for an intermittent spring to
shake our sorry heads together, half-wishing we
were elsewhere. To love or loathe this town isn't
the issue, of course. The key question is: when to
leave and for how long?

I took the advice of a lawyer lying slumped in
a second-hand bookshop tucked away in the
shadow of the David Hume Tower. Here, leaning
on the Brontë sisters to his left, and collecting a
layer of dark dust, I found James Boswell, eyes
and ears closed to the world, retreating to some
inner sanctuary of imagined indecency. Or so I
thought. As I passed, looking quizzically at him,
he burst into life, quoting Dr Johnson ardently:
"The noblest prospect which a Scotchman ever
sees, is the high road that leads him to England!"

I was taken aback, I admit, but engaged. "Well
Jamie," I thought, "times they change a little."
I had myself come back from London that
afternoon. What did returning to the city mean?
It was the faint smell of piss on Fleshmarket
Close as I left Waverley station, the sight of
cigarette butts, smoked that parsimonious bit
further down to the filter, and swimming in
puddles of rainwater. None of this was pleasant,
but it was familiar, it was unpretentious. That I
couldn't say about my new acquaintance. There
seemed good reason to suspect him; I could
never see directly into his eyes.

In any case I took him with me.

*

All evening he tried to persuade me to decamp permanently. Throw in my lot with an altogether better class of person, in a better class of city; that was how it seemed to him. All Scotsmen did it, either physically or mentally, he insisted, nodding to the landmarks of the university, its buildings all around us: "William Robertson, David Hume, Adam Smith! Andrew Neil!" he cried into the lowering darkness. "They deny this nation before they embrace it. North Britons, they try to call themselves. Submit, my boy! Rule Britannia was written by a Scot, don't forget. Submit!"

It was all too much. He had a way with words, but I wouldn't want to vote with the man. Luckily, that wasn't on the cards, and he dragged me to the High Street for a bottle of wine, and a round of banter to keep the evening's flame lit. He spoke of Rotterdam, Paris, and Corsica. How he discovered London at nineteen, drank his way around Europe meeting Voltaire and Rousseau, and was back in Edinburgh to join the bar and contract gonorrhoea seventeen times by his late twenties.

"So you knew you'd come back?" I asked.

He just ignored me, as usual, looking around the pub he'd found – the Mitre. He sat silent, and seemed to be changing his mind about something, or bringing back a painful memory. "There's a tavern like this in... In London there are men who would have us lose our tongues," he mumbled. "'You do not speak, Sir. You sing.' Or so I've been told."

Late into the night he kept walking, stopping, looking, and always talking. I tried to keep up with him, but he had more energy than I'd expected.

*

After that first, frenzied, meeting, I fancied that I would see Jamie on occasion as I walked through the city streets: leaning over a bar, long past closing-time, to fill a final glass, incoherent but voluble; strolling pompously out to dine with the Faculty of Advocates, an unashamed elitist, yet with an underlying passion for honesty and a distaste for intolerance. I played out the possible scenarios in my mind. Sometimes I would acknowledge him awkwardly and politely; more often I would conspicuously avoid him, ignore him. I don't feel guilty. We've never lived in the same city, anyhow, not really. So I shouldn't worry about bumping into him.

On one count, anyway, his example is a comfort. This son of a laird, with large and varied appetites from a young age, made it out and back. He left; he returned. I don't take it as a model, I just hold it as a truth.

Me? I'll stay put for now. Forsaking ambition and in fear of patriotism, I'll settle for a morning walk back to Pickering's bookshop, where I first met Jamie. There's something curious about those hours of the morning, a breath of summer on the breeze, an imagined future calling us forward. So light so early. Lost strangers drift through parks and down streets. It's dangerous to look them in the eye; to risk finding out what they are really thinking. Yet, the wider the jaws of night open, the more at home I feel.

Multiple Universes

By Karl Plume

"God does not play dice!"
Einstein averred to Bohr.
A statement which implies
Either that God is a bore,
That the quote is a fraud,
Or that the dice play God...

I'm not sure which option I least abhor.

Welcome To The Festival Of Fantasy

The Faerie Boy Of Leith

By Craig Gibson

The Master without Honour and a coterie of assorted Gun veterans were drinking earnestly in the Bailie Bar one balmy evening in late July. This was not a social occasion, and the faces around the table were grim as their owners discussed the latest snub to be delivered to The Gun by the all-powerful Edinburgh International Book Festival. Once again, Ms Catherine Lockerbie had refused permission for The Gun to be distributed FREE in the hallowed precincts of Charlotte Square Gardens. According to Frau Direktor, The Gun, an Edinburgh paper produced by and for the good people, had 'no direct link to the EIBF'. It was the opinion of those present that this insult must be avenged by any means necessary, but nevertheless the company realised that they could not achieve this goal on their own. To send The Gun against the EIBF in a toe-to-toe would be a brave, but ultimately doomed gesture and would accomplish nothing. After much debate the company agreed they would have to seek aid from elsewhere, for they could not stand alone against the ruthless corporate giant.

The Master's face suddenly took upon a crafty look and, although he feared ridicule for what he was about to suggest, he continued.

"Yes my friends, we need a powerful ally. Unfortunately, all the literary powers-that-be in town are in Catherine's pocket.

Therefore we must turn to another kind of aid. Something a bit out of the ordinary. Something supernatural," he hissed for dramatic effect. He was instantly mocked by the more rationalist members of the table, but he held up his hand and continued.

"My Grandad, who was a sailor, bequeathed to me on his deathbed a small wooden box containing a rude flute and a set of instructions written on vellum. These told of the Faerie Boy of Leith and described how the owner of the flute, in a time of crisis, could summon him if he stood on the Calton Hill when the moon was full and played a certain tune. Now, I know some of you may be familiar with Captain George Burton's account and assume it is nothing more than a fable. Well, my Grandad swore the Faerie Boy was for real and though he was a drinking man, he was never a liar. So, my friends, as it is full moon in three days time, I am going to take my flute up the Calton Hill at midnight and summon the help of all Faerieland!"

"You can't even play the flute!" the Fingersmith snorted, as the entire table broke up with guffaws and jeers.

"I'm a fucking quick learner," the Master retorted as he swept from the bar haughtily.

*

Calton Hill, full moon. The Master checked his watch and saw it was a quarter to the witching hour. Swiftly, he removed the flute from his inside pocket and laid the vellum gently on the ground. With the aid of his lighter he read through the instructions once again even though he had spent the previous three evenings memorising them. No point in taking any

104

chances, he thought. At the appointed time he turned around three times, widdershins, and began to play the simple tune as instructed on the manuscript. He was rather smugly congratulating himself on his new-found musical ability when he detected a slight whiff of sulphur, and sensed that someone was standing behind him. He whirled around to observe the Boy, who was shaking his head in a good natured, if slightly insolent fashion.

"Gled ye could mak it, Maister Falkland. No seen ye doon the Port for a lang time syne. The bodies say ye're an Edinburgh man noo," said the imp mischievously. "Noo whit can ah dee for ye?"

PERSEVERE

This was all a bit much for the Master to take in all at once, but he found his mouth working as if of its own accord.

"Why have you got a Borders accent if you're the Faerie Boy of Leith, then?"

"Ah kin talk like a Leither if that wid suit ye better. But I suspect that only the Queen's English will be good enough for the Master without Honour these days," the Boy sneered. He was about the same height as an 11-year-old child, but his upturned nose, pointy ears and tousled hair gave him a Puck-like appearance that befitted an ambassador from Faerieland. His drum hung carelessly at his side and he twirled the beaters idly in his left hand. He was, however, dressed in the manner of a contemporary urchin: hooded top, trackie bottoms and trainers. For some reason the Master found this apparel to be the most disconcerting thing of all.

"How do you know my name? And how do I know you're for real? Those don't look like Faerie clothes to me," he enquired, scratching his head. "You might be an impostor."

"I know many things, my good Master," said the imp impatiently, "for I've been here a long, long time." His voice and manner belied his youthful appearance. "And I dress how I please. Tracksuits and the like are very comfortable," he stated curtly. His little flinty eyes narrowed suspiciously. "I know your name and I know why you've come, for I read you as easily as a book. You want me to bang my drum and have the whole Faerie Host descend upon Charlotte Square Gardens for the month of August. Think of it, a horde of invisible brownies and bogles, kelpies and pisgies, imps and elves, all pulling at guy-ropes, ruining readings, salting the beer, invading the Writers' Yurt and tweaking their noses, pulling their hair and stealing children. The Host unleashed against the EIBF, that is what you desire, is it not?" The Master's eyes were afire as he nodded.

"Then you are a fool and your arrogance will be your undoing. You really thought that by playing a few notes, badly I may add, on your Grandad's flute you could command the Invisible Empire to do your bidding!" The imp went into a fit of giggles that threatened to transform him into a child again. The Master stared at his feet, his face reddening, feeling more foolish than ever. The Boy recovered his composure and stared curiously at him as he began to turn away dejectedly. "Hey, come back here. Don't be so downhearted. You have summoned me and I am here to help you. So listen and learn. But first of all, give me a roll-up."

*

"Revenge, my good Master, is a dish best served cold," said the Faerie Boy as he puffed contentedly on his hand-made, "and in any case I am going to put such foolish notions out of your head by using a cunning blend of magic and common sense. Come." The Boy led the Master to the highest point of the hill before proceeding, much to the Master's bemusement, to piss into a small hollow, whistling all the while. A phenomenal amount of piss for one so small, mused the Master, as the Boy took at least three minutes to complete this task. The Boy let out a long, theatrical sigh of pleasure and delved his hand deeply into his pocket before bringing out a tightly clenched fist.

"Real Faerie Dust, Master Falkland, just like in

the books," teased the Boy, his eyes twinkling as he opened his hand to allow the silver substance to fall like a miniature snowstorm over the lochan of piss at his feet. "Now look into the mirror and tell me what you see." The Master stepped forward dubiously and gazed into the puddle. At first all he could see was his own form with the moon behind him. However, this image gradually faded to be replaced by a scene that he knew all too well. A miniscule Charlotte Square Gardens in the sunshine. He could not help but be astonished by this spectacle and he stood transfixed by the sight of a teeny Catherine Lockerbie leading a tiny Jamie Byng by the arm in the direction of a diminutive Writers' Yurt.

"The Book Festival. The fucking Book Festival!" gasped the Master looking up. "But tell me – which festival am I looking at? Last year's, or this which has still to pass?"

"Ha! Then you've already grasped the first lesson. You can't tell, can you? As a matter of fact, nor can I. You see – same shit, different year. Same tents, corporate logos, same old faces doing the rounds. The garden mobbed as usual. Maybe you understand a bit better now. Look into the mirror again – the EIBF is strictly a 'bums on seats, laddie' organisation. A winning formula you might say, and one of which The Gun has no part. You have nothing to offer that is of any value to them. That's it, stare into the mirror and face the truth. The Gun is a free press, a gift to literary Edina, and as the EIBF's entire philosophy appears to involve nothing more than vulgar commerce, you are anathema to them."

The Boy swept his hand over the mirror and the vision vanished. The Master shook his head slowly and smoked a pipe of pot thoughtfully whilst the Faerie Boy helped himself to more tobacco. After a few minutes silence the Master was forced to admit that the Boy had it sussed and expressed this verbally.

"What are we to do then?" he enquired.

"With regard to the festival? Nothing at all. In fact go and see a few shows, maybe. I would recommend Rushdie – that man's got balls. Above all, don't let it spoil your fun or interfere with your mission. The month of August can bear fruit if you look in the right places. Seek and ye shall find etcetera. With regards to The Gun, as a Leith man you should know this – persevere!

"I don't like to prophecy for it can addle the mind sometimes, but I can tell you a few things. You and your colleagues are going to enjoy the ride if you stick to the true path, and you will be a happy man before your beard is grey. The Gun has endured many trials during its brief life – treachery, jealousy, poverty, and indifference, to name but a few. These trials have only strengthened the resolve and integrity of all involved. You will succeed on your own terms, but you must persevere!"

"Can you show me our future in the mirror?" asked the Master eagerly and with much anticipation.

"No. Too much too soon, I'm afraid. To look upon that would be akin to looking upon the face of the Most High – for such knowledge would burn you! Just heed my words, laddie. Keep the faith and above all persevere! Now listen to these Leithers who succeeded on their own terms." With these words the Boy took a step back and began to beat out a simple rhythm upon his drum. The beat became infectious and the Master, despite himself, started clapping his hands enthusiastically as the Boy began to sing The Joyful Kilmarnock Blues by the Proclaimers. However, to the Master's delight, it was the voice of Craig Reid that issued from the Boy. And wait – was it just the wind or could he really hear Charlie's backing vocals and guitar? The Master closed his eyes rapturously and joined in with gusto.

I'm not going to talk about doubts and confusion
On a night when I can see with my eyes shut

The wisdom of Craig and Charlie had long been held sacred by the Master and his voice soared as they chanted the lyrics together.

The question doesn't matter
The answer's always 'aye'
The best view of all
Is where the land meets the sky

As the song drew to a close, the Master found himself drowsy and he was unable to combat the waves of tiredness which had begun to overwhelm him. More Faerie magic, he thought contentedly. He lay down, and as he drifted off, the last thing he heard was the Boy gently murmuring in his Borders voice:

"Ah'll have tae leave ye noo, Maister Falkland. But ah'll leave ye a wee token as ye've been a very clever chiel. Ye'll persevere noo, mind." The Master awoke at dawn and was immediately aware of an object lying at his feet. 'Twas a beautiful Pringle sweater with a red body, midnight-blue sleeves and boasting a lion rampant for decoration on the chest. On closer inspection, the Master discovered that the sweater had been signed by the brothers

Reid and bore the legend PERSEVERE! This garment was far too precious to be worn on any man's back, he judged. Instead, he would mount the Boy's gift on a T-bar and use it as the Gun standard, just like the Faerie Flag of Dunvegan. It would serve them well in the coming month. As the Master left the hill clutching his precious memento, he was reminded of the children's programme Mr Benn and allowed himself a brief chuckle: God knows what the others are going to make of this...

Editor's Note: Any reader who would like to peruse Captain George Burton's original account of the Faerie Boy of Leith, as related to Richard Bovet, gentleman, can find the tale with little effort on the World Wide Web. The Faerie Flag of The Gun can be observed at any Gun launch party, or on occasions where our cause requires a little magical aid.

Letters

Dear Gun,

As you lie there in your damp camp, steeling
yourself for yet more of the dismal science of
office life and a further dose of pique from all
the petty hells your colleagues port about like
odours in their narrow minds, I ask you to spare
a thought for me, blindfolded like a condemned
soldier, contemplating a whole week of reading.

Blindfold and a last cigarette? Picture my
trepidation, my black-spiked angst, picture my
hot sudation as you lie awake in your financial
hell. I apologise for my last letter – you send me
out for a melodeon and I return with two snipe
and a half pound of barley-sugar. Charming.
I still need to write to you however, a product
perhaps of extreme cabin fever, but a usual
means of fulfilling (one of!) Robert Burton's
dicta: that the melancholy man should try as
much as possible to push negative thoughts aside
by means of the positive, however nebulous and
chimerical. As good old Seneca says:

'As meat is to the body, such is reading to the
soul.'

And Cardano says:

'To be at leisure without books is another hell
and to be buried alive. A library is physic for the
soul.'

And St Jerome prescribed Rufinus the Monk:

' – continually to read and to meditate on that
which you hath read, for as mastication is to
meat, so is meditation on that which we read.'

And Heinsius, Keeper of the University Library
at Leyden stated:

'I no sooner come into the library, but I bolt the
door excluding lust, avarice, ambition and all
such vices – I take my seat with so lofty a spirit
and sweet content that I pity all our great men
and rich that know not this happiness.'

Yours from his bookish cell,

Raymondo

Sour Grapes

By Martin Hillman

Ram, Boar and Stag had to sit at Fox's table
because the canteen was full. They would have
liked to sit at one of the tables where the birds
were and wear their tee-shirts, shaven heads
and pierced ears but they had to sit with Fox
where they were just blokes in tight, slightly too
light clothes with earrings and square, bumpy
skulls. They left the seats next to and facing Fox
empty.

They had large quantities of salad in addition to
their chips. Their drinks were all diet and lite.

"Give us the salt, mate," Ram said to Fox.

Fox was not listening, so Ram reached over for it.
Fox continued reading.

The salt was empty so Ram said: "Pass us that
other salt, will you mate."

Fox woke up just in time to pass it before Ram's
muscly arm with a band tattooed round it could
push past him. "Increases blood pressure, salt,"
said Fox. "Increased risk of strokes."

"I don't mind getting strokes," said Ram. "If
chicks give me strokes in the right place, it gets
bigger and stronger."

Boar took a great slug of low-fat milk. Fox
said: "That's probably got breast-development
hormone in it, you know."

"Don't worry about me, mate," said Boar. "I've
been working on my pecs."

Stag ate a forkful of lettuce and spring onions. Fox said: "Have you any idea about the amount of insecticide they have to put on that stuff to keep productivity per acre up? Why do you think the average sperm count's falling so fast?"

"I've never screwed a chick yet that's wanted to count my sperm," said Stag.

Ram drank some sugar-free, low-calorie cola. Fox said: "The sweetener in that messes up your head. It makes kids hyperactive."

"My bird likes it when I'm hyperactive," said Ram.

Boar put chips on his slice of white bread and took a huge mouthful. Fox said: "Have you thought about the..."

"Low-fat oven chips, soft-grain bread for roughage, and low-cal sunflower-oil marge," said Boar. "Matey."

Stag started on a tub of rice pudding which came packed with a subsidiary tub of jam in one corner. Fox started to speak but Stag interrupted him: "What you had for your lunch anyway, matey?"

"Just some mineral water," said Fox, and just as the other three were about to start mocking, the colleague he had been waiting for came past and they went off.

"God, my stomach," said Fox to his friend. "We were on tequila last night and then someone had a bottle of one of those pepper vodkas." But he was already looking forward to the evening: he was planning steak and then strawberries and cream. His weight was steady, he bought organic dairy products and he had had a vasectomy years ago.

A Wee Visit

By Graham Brodie

I am in this building
Waiting for you
Come and see me

I have been here
Since the collection
Began

I am in a jar
My body is crushed
In to a small gallery

I have flipper feet
But I cannot swim anywhere
I am trapped

I am a part of my brother
Whose head looks
At you too

I am older than him
More
beautiful

Will you come
And see me please?
I am alive

Come to Surgeons' Hall
For a visit
Say hello with girlfriend or wife

A day out in the sun
An ice cream
Melting

I feel you hold hands
And laugh as you
Look

It is nice to have
A wee visit
Once in a while

Sketches Of London

The Clergyman Abroad

By Andrew Smith

As I sit in the cold parlour of a semi-detached
terraced house in Wimbledon, I take no delight
in either tea or scone. The reason? I hear the
trains passing beneath on the District Line.
I hear their clickety-clack, clickety-clack (was
there ever a sound more suggestive of carnal
activity!), and I know full well the destination
of these shameless locomotives. They speed
northeastwards towards London, and towards
a totem of profanity! There is a structure,
which I can barely bring myself to identify by
name, which towers newly above the London
landscape, a profane silhouette against the
skyline, mocking the austere majesty of St
Paul's, which the pious Wren created in honour
of the Almighty. I speak indeed about the
headquarters of a certain insurance company
(Ha! Moneylenders!). In stature and shape it
is a vile obelisk, suggesting to men both good
and bad the form of an unmentionable bodily
organ, turgid with lurid fluids and lustfulness.
This building is decreed by demonic will to utter
offence to the Christian sensibility. The men that
created such audacious paganism, conceiving
of this obscenity of steel and glass and ungodly
elements, are clearly bereft of modesty or belief
in Scripture. They shall be damned. I can only
pray that such evils will never pervade our great
Scottish capital – ah, dear city! – and darken the
moral substance of our good citizens. Travelling
as I have been, it is many years since I trod the
close and stair of fair Edinburgh, and I hear news
of a House of Scottish Parliament newly erected
near the Holyrood Park, with its invigorating air

and views seaward. I need hardly say that – and I have no doubts in this matter – the architect of this new Scottish establishment will be a Scot of modest and Godly belief, who will build us a house befitting our sobriety and piety, with thrift and haste and causing no bother to the purse of the city. Of this I am most sure.

The Road To Go Where

By Barry McLaren

It's over, Rover. Irish, Irish eyes are smiling,
many, green, green miles from here. And these
fertile shamrocks dilute this fear. And here,
here I am willing head in willing hand willing my
shoes to see it through, all the way to away from
you. The surrounding, grey skies hurtle Irish
signals from across the sea to here, three miles
in on the road to Stranraer from Port Patrick,
from where once the charmed wooden ferry took
Irish muscles to a promised land of money in the
pocket ending in late night bar-room tussles. To
the left of the road upon a grassy hill stands a
telephone mast replacing the busier past.

Twelve white circles,
Catching voices in the wind,
Preaching and teachings
From the angels and the sinned.

Hell was easy, but not this breezy. Walking up
the road with the firing shots of horizontal Irish
H2O, driving me onwards, to a destination of
a desolate nation, which may or may not open
up in front of me. Now I once heard Stranraer
described as the 'arsehole of Scotland' by a duct
engineer from Fife. That seems to be poignant
in my mind as I feel nothing to my rear, too cold,
too wet. Got to go to go to get.

Wet trance
Rain dance
Wet pants
Inching France.

How far to Stranraer? Don't know, I skipped the
pain and got the train. Scotrail is an acute form

of purple depression, that ain't a fact, on track,
just my impression. A soggy man in a metal
can. The Bonnie Ailsa Craig passes the time as
she swings into/out of view, watching her pass
in a mechanical pew; she's the elegant maritime
mountain of mine. As we come to a predictable
stop, metal grinds metal; eventually we settle
five miles short of Ayr on this klutz of a ride that
ain't no funfair, unfair. "I would like to apologise
on behalf of Scotrail, we are experiencing
delays ahead and will keep you updated as to an
expected time of arrival." I'll just have to bury
my head in the sand(wich). I pray, no further
delay, today.

Rabbie Burns
In his grave he turns
At the purple waste
of time we spurn

Onwards, I don't remember what I was doing
down thon way in Galloway, all I remember is
that I just couldn't stay another day, a mental
price to pay, no concession, just my impression.
Glesga beckons, me reckons, I'm a man of the
mountains, get me out of here. Johnstone and
Paisley go by, my eastern eye. And the Scottish
planes depart to bluer skies like homing flies.
The industrial landscape scrapes the windows as
Metropol Caledonia swamps the view, Orange
flickers, Ned's knickers, Metallic air and concrete
sinew. "Whit de ye want?" Night falls like an
orange filled black curtain at Central station, it's
a sign, an indication. Onwards and Northwards
to the poetic hills and the Caledon fjords. Where
sheep are sheep and Lords are Lords. Through
the gauntlet I go, fearlessly so, I daren't be
slow. It's the Saturday night Sauchiehall Street
sideshow. Frowns to the left of me, smokers to
the right, here I am stuck in the middle with you,
Superman, handing me a flyer for all night cheap

vodka at Majestik's. Ahead three drunkards get
another two arrested. The wild mare screams
at random old him for a kiss he detested. A
teenager spews a kebab he wished he'd digested.
My feet get the message as they slide on through
the mad, soggy view. I got to head west, for a
one-night rest, take the pedal bike north, that's
what's best is best. I hope it's blue tomorrow.

Dark clouds
In the dead of night
Shifted by the wiggely-woggely men
Atlantic winds
Clear the sins
And seagulls sleep in bins
Well where else do they sleep?
Black
Orange tinge
Purple
Giving way to blue
Crystal clear
Crisp, crisp blue
Good for me
And good for you.

Aluminium alloy spinning toy. Paniers packed,
wheels trimmed, second city of the empire is
sacked, stay slim. Feet cycling round and round
and around, sonic receptacles blocking post-
industrial sounds, rubbered rip of a two-wheeled
ship part of the circle rhythmically pressing the
ground. The invisible print in invisible tint mark
one memory. I am off to Queen Street station to
catch the train to Oban if I can.

The Hour Of The Witch

*formerly known as The Nineteen
Joys Of The Mad Virgin*

By Suhayl Saadi

It is the hour of the witch, the moment of
knowledge. By the trunk of the blackthorn tree,
the Witch Queen holds between her teeth the
balls of the kiss'd, blinded dominie of oak and
she feels the life slip from his body as his shadow
rushes to the rough ground beneath her feet.
The sky turns gold, red and black. She lays him
down on the fire, anoints herself with the salt
of his skin, then leaps over the cauldron eight
times, once for each garter, and then in the green
smoke of his flesh, she begins to dance in a circle.
She dances slowly at first like a molten stream,
but with each deosil sweep of her white arm, her
feet move faster and faster until she is wheel-
kicking antiphons over the arc of her skull, and
then, in a moment of perfect, farishta circularity,
the balls fly from the clamp of her jaw and whirl
through the air, and land on her feet, each ball
rolling on the tip of a big ox toe. And now, she,
the balls and the wind swirl into a blur and
occupy all points at once.

Then she rises and flies as a wheel across the
willow forest and the moors of red heather and
the teeming city of lions, and guided by the
eagle of Yahya, she crosses the cold blue sea
to the island of summer where words spiral in
poetry up mountain-goat tracks. The vomiting
dragon grants her passage over the bridge, and
the octagonal House of Aradia welcomes her
within its magic walls of cedar, sandalwood and
juniper. Still cradling the balls of the king in

123

the epidermal forest of her foot-skins, the witch
eats the food of the dumb supper, she drinks
from barrels of mead, she hears trumpless music
which has no sound, no notes and she bathes
in wine which evaporates slowly from her skin
into the air. She is scourg'd by the tail'd cat and
bleeds vines into the earth and, as joyous fireflies
pour down in light upon her, still she dances
between the peaks of song.

At matins, her hair has grown long and has
clothed her body in its black cloak, and she is
whirling widdershins on a dark hill, and her
fingers have lengthened and they pluck wrens
from the boughs of ancient oaks, and the blood
of the wrens feeds her belly which has bladder'd
across the hog valley, so that as her spine writhes
in the dance, she lies down upon a blossom
couch, and from her raised, opened thighs, leap
eleven wild skeletons. And the skeletal women
sing lauds in a chorus-line:

Horse and hattock, horse and go!

Horse and pellatis, ho, ho, ho!

They sing this eleven times and their words raise
a bone fire into the sky and the witch rocks on
her rolling heels so that her feet become the long
cone of a demon horse, head-to-claw, and the
prime demon takes aim and kicks the balls of
the King into the heart of the flames. The world
stops. Breath ceases. Terce.

Then, from the heart of the fire, there leaps a
giant, horn'd god. Peacock'd, bulbous, sext.
And the Witch Queen is unmoving, none, as the
beast lies down upon her and the two take up
the chorea of electric blue quivering stillness and
their glowing, vespering transparency becomes
a line of litanic fire which cuts compline into

the ground to form a spherical, glass altar. And through the glass, the Witch Queen sees the dark bone arch of the new moon, omphalos in the magenta sack of the sky. And in the black mirror of Idris, she calls past the cist and reads everything that has happ'd and everything that will come.

Mistress of the Mountains,
Shahzadi Junoon of Farax

The Death Of The Philosopher

By James Mooney

The Laird of Newington Manor was wintering
at his country estate and the new university
term was yet to begin in earnest. Accordingly,
the Philosopher had been alone for some
weeks. His insistence that potential visitors
first contact him by telephone, alongside his
resistance to answering the intrusive device, had
led, as was his intention, to no-one darkening
his doorstep. Even the once regular death-bell
of the unanswered telephone had lapsed into
an occasional death-rattle, before expiring
completely.

This self-induced exile had become a necessary
ritual in the Philosopher's life. Each year, in
the midst of the Festival of Darkness, he seized
the opportunity for change. This change,
however, was not of the type easily bought with
a mere resolution. What was required was a
revolution – the overthrow of his previous self
in its entirety. He would address himself to the
general upheaval of all his former principles and
would strive to create himself anew. It was thus
necessary that he should strip himself bare of
the transient relationships he had made since
his last cleansing. Only in this way could he
separate the essential from the incidental. Only
through solitude can you realise true authenticity
and freedom of the Will.

The process had been an unsettling one, more
so than in years gone by. The threat of nihilism
hung heavy in the air and the Philosopher
felt empty and devoid of purpose. Then came
the call, though it took some time for him to
recognise the once familiar sound. He answered

in a muffled tone, lest it should be someone he had no desire to converse with. In this way he could feign illness, or even mistaken identity, and make his escape. However, he need not have feared. Fortuna had just presented him with an ideal opportunity for re-evaluation and self-creation, in the form of a launch party for a self-styled satirical magazine.

He arrived fashionably late – in truth, it had taken him some time to perfect his costume. He had settled on last year's black, which he was fairly confident would remain this year's black. Only two utterances were made on the journey – "Travesty Bar please" and "Keep the change" – the latter as recompense for the lack of any others. As he sauntered down the stairs and towards the bar the Philosopher reminded himself of the importance of the evening. As a result, he would have to curtail his excessive drinking – and opiates were certainly out of the question. The purpose of the night was not, after all, recreational, but foundational.

He ordered his drink, chose a table on the periphery which afforded him a fine vista, and picked up the publication. For the next hour he sipped at his drink and tossed down the offering of 'Gun-Lite' which poured from the pages in front of him. As he read, he felt his Will begin to rise and swell. He ordered another drink and leant back in his seat to survey the scene around him. Observing the populace of the bar he was reminded of Plato's noble lie: that some were made with gold in the soul, some with silver, and some bronze. And those with souls of gold, the 'philosopher kings', states Plato, are intended to reign over the others. Aristotle too, the great categoriser, speaks of a natural inequality in men; 'From the hour of birth', he says, 'some are marked out for subjection, others for rule.'

As the Philosopher considered the Greeks he felt his Will surge. A multitude of thoughts swirled through his mind. From Rousseau's paranoid romanticism and his conjecture that some must be 'forced to be free' – a thought only brought to fruition with the aid of Madame Guillotine – he moved on to Nietzsche's bifurcation of humanity into Übermensch and Untermensch. The German's indictment of contemporary society as a place in which Aristotle's natural order had become inverted and limitations were placed on the will of higher men as a result of the slave revolt reverberated in the Philosopher's soul. He broke off from his introspection to survey once again the words on the pages in front of him and the world around him. As he did so, he felt like a One O'Clock Gulliver at the Lilliputian launch: it would take thousands of these fuckers to bring me down, he thought.

The Philosopher's thoughts turned to the Master without Honour – he must let him know of these revelations. He attempted to contact him by telephone, but to no avail. The Philosopher consoled himself with the thought that the Master was either engaged in important Gun business, or that he too was seeking the solitude necessary for rebirth. As he prepared to leave, however, Fortuna once again spun her wheel in his direction, and the Master breezed into the bar. They ordered drinks and both returned to the table where the Philosopher informed the Master of his mission and its success. After a few more glasses and no little plotting, the Philosopher promised the Master a full written account of the evening's events and took his leave.

As he strode purposefully across the Meadows toward home, the Philosopher was accompanied by the words of Zamyatin. The Russian, too,

PLATE I: Homemade wooden boxes containing the One O'Clock Gun were a feature of many of Edinburgh's bars. Above: The Pear Tree House proudly displays a box on its mantlepiece underneath a portrait of Burns.

PLATE II: The first ever edition. The basic cross-fold system was useful but we knew that more could be made of this format.

PLATE III: Number 2. The cunning folds which would become a Gun standard appear for the very first time.

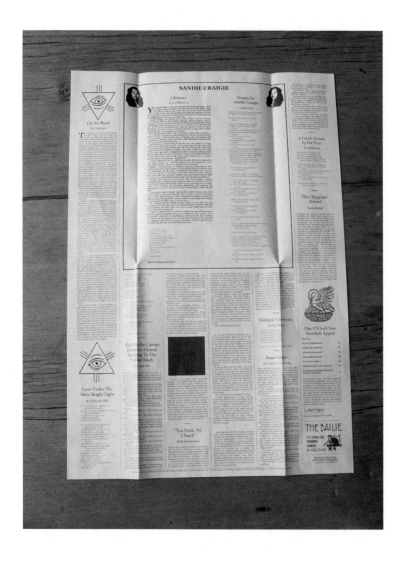

Plate iv: The back of Number 6. Here we commemorate Edinburgh poet Sandy Craigie – sadly this would be not be the last time we honoured Edinburgh's fallen.

PLATE V: A facsimile of the front of Number 7, illustrating Volume II's new name and masthead.

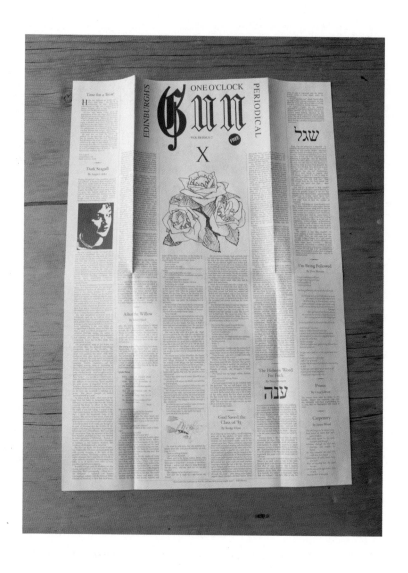

PLATE VI: The front page of Number 10 featuring a return to the full title and another new masthead.

PLATE VII: Detail from the reverse of Number 10; the first publication of a play in the Gun, Alasdair Gray's Goodbye Jimmy and the first time a Gun page was printed horizontally.

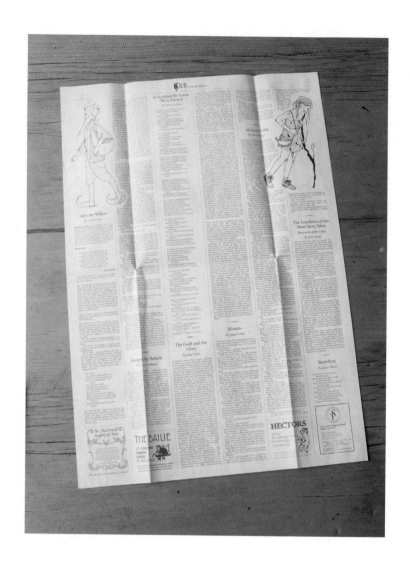

PLATE VIII: The back page of Number 11 reverts to the now-familiar format.

PLATE IX: Obverse of Number 12, showing Gerry Hillman (designer) and Craig Gibson (editor). Have no doubts about self-promotion in this business — it's the only type of promotion that is fully guaranteed.

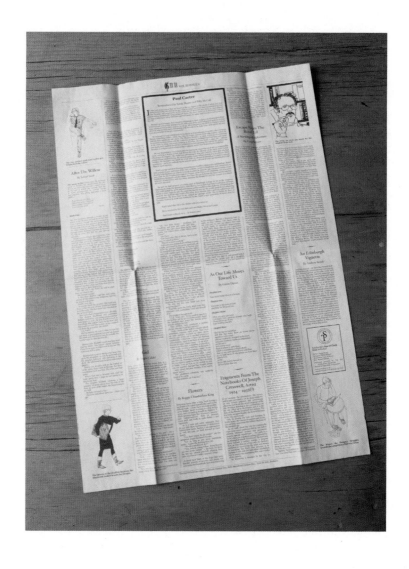

PLATE X: A further obituary as the Gun salutes artist and lecturer Paul Carter (1970 – 2006) on the reverse of Number 12.

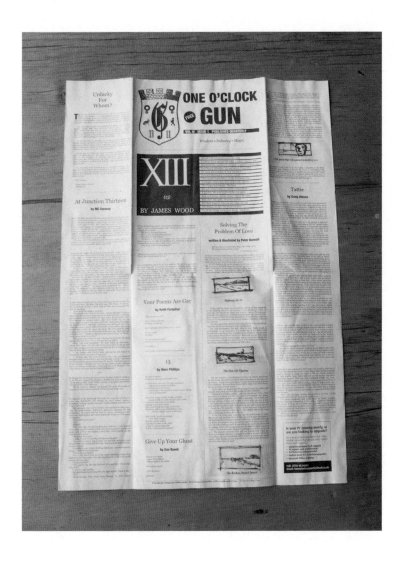

PLATE XI: A well thumbed copy of OOCG Number 13. A new volume, a new masthead and a new slogan: Wisdom – Industry – Magic.

PLATE XII: The front of Number 16, the final issue of Volume IV. The last Gun to be seen in Edinburgh taverns for some time.

PLATE XIII: The reverse of Number 16, featuring the work of Gun regular Sandy Christie.

PLATE XIV: Number 17, the infamous Duality edition. The Gun now had more admirers and fewer friends than ever.

PLATE XV: The abuse continues on the reverse of Number 17. We also bid a fond farewell to another Gun regular, Angus Calder (1942 – 2008).

PLATE XVI: Tweed, steel and soul: an alchemist's dream. Gun Editor Gibson at the One O'Clock Gun Exhibition, Edinburgh Castle, March 2010.

Photographs by Robin Gillanders
Except Plate I Tommy Grace
And Plate XVI OOCG Collection

speaks of this world as populated by different types; there are, he claims, not only the living and the dead, but the living dead, and the latter can be identified by their attempts to eliminate suffering, that component most vital to the flourishing will. The Philosopher considered his own suffering, and as he did, he felt the gold coursing through his veins. He was reborn. Or rather, I was born – Oliver Twisted, the Leading Light of the Bitterati. "The Philosopher is dead, long live the Philosopher King!" I cried into the night. This would be the year for the living to live, the wilful to thrive, and the masters to rule. And as for the rest – the slaves, the herd, the bungled and the botched, the many too many – let the dead bury the dead!

Rev Burneto On The Holy Isle

During the Reverend's most recent visit, the
Inquisitor for the Diocese of Durham, Roger
the Bugger, was persecuting the heretics of
Lindisfarne. Amongst the grievous errors
punished with the full force of the secular arm,
under the supervision of Seneschal Hughes
the Plank, were the Touching Cloth (otherwise
known as the Poor of Andrexis), the Tête de
Turtle, and the Abominable Modemsians, whose
failure to reply promptly to email has gained
for them the profound and lasting vexation of
the docta cyberalises. Of the total population of
the island of Lindisfarne at the time of visiting,
49% were found to be in error and the smoke for
the burnings, it is said, will still be visible from
space some seven months from now. Further, it
is believed to this day by the credulous dwellers
in Northumberland that visitors to the Holy Isle
who fail to reach the sanctuary of the Public
Toilets by the Castle before they excrete, will
inevitably run up large bills in the new Pants R
Us in the village. It is rumoured, by two sub rosa
homosexuals of Lindisfarne, that the locals put
dangerous quantities of laxative in the famous
mead as a belated revenge on all outsiders,
incomers, bypassers and overfliers. Lindisfarne
is not notorious for its furious partying and
the Rev Burneto was therefore asked to kindly
refrain from smiling or otherwise provoking
anti-capitalist riots while visiting. The penalties
for using joy in public are severe and include
Jim Davidson deployed at random, and the
imposition of compulsory Newcastle United.

A Night At The Highlander

A despatch from 'The Barman'

By Robin Vandome

It is the privilege of the hero's servant, a perceptive historian has observed, to witness great men when they are merely men. So, too, it is the privilege of the modern bartender to witness mere men appropriate the air of the great. Not so, of course, if one enters the Highlander (as was), a chameleon watering hole on the southern side of the city; here, rather than among the parades of fakers and pretenders in the New Town, one may mingle with the great and the good of Scottish culture, the genuine stalwarts of our national literary and musical tradition. They sit anonymous, lifting from the immaculate chrome bar frosted martini glasses, chilled pints of Tennents, and heavy brown bottles of Magners to their lips, and sigh, thinking of Yeats.

Take this chance meeting of two Glaswegian culture-smiths propping up the bar in the end-of-term slump: it occasioned a unique and almost violent contretemps, when new and old Scotland, the post and the pre-industrial, clashed head-on, from opposite ends of the zeitgeist. I watched from behind the bar, slowly emptying the glass washer and polishing the cocktail shaker.

Besuited, with a Humphrey Bogart tie slung inelegantly from his acne-scarred neck, Alex Kapranos entered soon after 8pm. Edinburgh? For a drink? Oh God, we have to! I watched as he kicked the mud off his boots and laid his duffle-coat over the bar stool.

The former ska-merchant, mercury flowing dangerously in his bloodstream, took full advantage of the two-for-one cocktail offer, and ordered one black Russian, and one cosmopolitan for his impish and beautiful female companion. These served – exquisitely, I might add, by myself, the final touch being the casual flick of a flambéed sliver of orange rind into the cosmo – the couple set up stall at the bar, furtively soaking up imagined stares of adoration from the Louis Vuitton cap-wearing regulars at the nearest table, one of whom, I believe, shouted "Oi! Cunt features! Fancy a swedge?"

"Edinburgh's fabulous," Alex intoned gravely, back turned to the ungracious hoi polloi. "People here think they have a night-life. Have you ever been out here before?" he asked the kitten on his arm.

No, she had not.

"We have to. It's so awful."

The girl smiled with an alarming level of excitement. Alex continued: "We'll go to Bertie's. I'll get beaten up; it'll be so good. If only Stuart was here. But he had to go to that seminary in Dumfries... "

Flinching from the urge to punch him square on the nose, I pulled a pint of Blackthorn for a regular, and was suddenly distracted by a minor kerfuffle at the door. Pushing his way inside, a greying and compact gentleman of advancing years had evidently become disaffected with the University's naked twister society pub-crawl congregating at the entrance. He made his solitary way to the bar, and a spare stool next to Mr Kapranos.

132

Sat uncomfortably, James Kelman quickly caught my eye; his request, I admit, knocked me off my stride a little.

"A Bacardi breezer. Lime."

"Right away."

What had brought the greatest living Scottish writer back to these shores, I wondered. Perhaps he had disgraced himself terribly at the creative writing school in America where he held a chair, after indulging in an all-night Johnnie Walker binge with Christopher Hitchens, shitting himself publicly in front of his colleagues and students. No, that was unlikely. For whatever reason, Kelman had also designated the Highlander as his drinking den of choice for the early evening, and I for one was delighted. Precisely the stripe of customer I wanted to encourage. Breezer in hand, he unflipped a carton of Lambert & Butler, and pawed fruitlessly at his pockets.

"Do you need a light?" Kind Alex, generous Alex.

"Aye – some capitalistfuckingguardianreading prick at the socalleduniversityofenglandburgh nicked off with my matches that I had lefted in the restaurant. On the table, just like that. And someone thought I wouldn't note the loss. Thank you."

Alex proffered a marvellous (I admit) Saddam Hussein lighter, the flame erupting from the tip of the tiny rifle he clutched to his chest, and Mr Kelman permitted himself a knowing laugh at the object.

"I like it, my boy."

133

"Thanks, I got it when we toured in Serbia."

"Is that right? So you're a performer of some kind?"

Kapranos, snubbed by anonymity, strained to conceal his displeasure. "Erm, yes. I sing in a band. Franz – "

"Ahh – Kafka! You know, I ache daily at being wedded to that giant's reputation."

"…"

"So," continued Kelman, warming to the edgy literary banter. "How explicitly political can art be? What, in your case, do you bring to the establishmentbastardpolitical world through your creativity?"

Kapranos' companion held Kelman in a glazed stare. I breathed heavily, waiting for the response.

Kelman supped on his breezer, Kapranos began to speak, though beads of unhip sweat were beginning to penetrate his unfeasible fringe. He began: "Y'know... I think it's important. But we're not about that. Statements are... Things happen the same way they always have. Change... change is possible; only... only the man who does nothing makes no mistakes... Y'know..."

Kelman's eyes narrowed, two piercing dots of radical intensity. "You fuckwit. An unknowing snippet of Lenin will get you nowhere but the dole queue. The bastards are powerful enough, we don't need some fucker like you helping them." He turned to me.

"And what do you think, worker?"

I considered my response carefully, but fluster took over, and, picking up an ashtray to wipe dry, I whispered meekly: "I'm – I'm sorry. I couldnay git thru Translated Accounts. I haven't started You Have To Be Careful yet either. 'Specially not after the unenthusiastic LRB review... I... I... "

The great man shook his head silently, looked down at the bar, and asked, too repulsed by me, by us all, to meet our gazes, "Well, could I have another fuckin' breezer then at least?"

Billy Semple

A Vignette

By Alasdair Gray

Leaning heavily on a stick and walking with
great difficulty, a man came into the pub where
I usually drink. I didn't think he was drunk but
the barman refused to serve him. The man said,
"I'm Billy Semple. I used to play for Rangers.
My legs are all shattered."

The barman said: "Sorry, but you can't drink
here. You'd better leave."

"How?"

"The way you came."

Both were silent for a while then the barman
asked if he should phone for a taxi. Semple
nodded.

While the barman phoned I helped Semple to
the door and stood outside with him, though
standing seemed as hard for him as walking. I
then noticed he was very drunk indeed. I know
nothing about football, so to make conversation
said: "Not easy, eh?" He muttered something
like, "You never know how things will end."

The taxi arrived but when the driver saw Semple
he said, "Not in my cab," and drove off. I went
back into the pub and told the barman to phone
for an ambulance. He did and came outside.
The three of us waited and when the ambulance
came the ambulance men also refused to take
Semple. I hadn't realised our health services
now reject helpless invalids for being drunk, but

of course the world keeps changing all the time.

"Nothing for it but the police," said the barman going inside. And when the police came they lifted Semple into their van and drove off.

End of story. Maybe they charged him with being drunk and disorderly, maybe they took him to wherever he lived, maybe both. I asked someone who is a big football fan if he had heard of Billy Semple. He said: "Yes. Used to play for Rangers. Definitely a name to conjure with."

Maybe the man was lying about his name. I am sure he was not.

My Gode

By Karl Plume

Fuck you, God, you silly cunt!
Your mediocre architecture does not impress;
This art installation you freely flaunt
Is no better than a potter in a dress.

I know that such an attack demands
An old man on a cloud, or a sacred mist,
For how can one slip one's hands
Around a throat which does not exist?

But if, by some slightest chance, a
God is extant, and I've incurred his wrath
With a candid though somewhat vulgar stanza:
I fancy the paving shall be superior on the fiery
    path!

So this is now my nightly cant:
Fuck you, God, you silly cunt!

Aux Armes, Citoyens!

By Angus Calder

Eventually, in those days when I 'taught literature', I reached the point where I told my Open University students: "If it isn't witty or beautiful, don't bother to read it." Implying that I didn't want to inspect yet more essays earnestly prospecting for moral lessons in Huck Finn, forsooth, forfucksake, or imposing off-the-peg 'literary theory' or 'gender theory' on Mrs Dalloway without regard for Woolf's delicious prose. (Virginia can. Jacques Lacan't.)

One has to be careful, though, to refine both terms. 'Wit' has nothing to do with fall-about ha-ha on TV chat shows. It refers to the pleasure given by the unpredictable the application of intelligence. 'Beauty' does not depend on pretty subject matter. Someone might write beautifully about pizza vomited on to a pavement under streetlights. Wit generates fresh thoughts. Beauty cleans our vision. To achieve either wit or beauty (or both at once – this can be done – see Andrew Marvell, or Beckett), technique is required. A sentence must prance, or saunter or stride, not plod. No verse is free (TS Eliot put it thus) for a man who wants to do a good job. The battering of wives in Blackhall could be an important subject for a TV documentary or newspaper feature. But a plodding novel about it will be the reverse of important. Description of the beauties of Argyll may serve the hotel trade well in the travel supplement. But a merely descriptive poem about any one of them is guaranteed to be quite awful.

Good writing of any kind happens when words intersect with our actual world in an unexpected way, not to reflect it, but, with a life of their own, to change our sense of it. It should not be relevant (therefore subservient) to society. It should, and does, work to reconstruct society.

A further caveat. Both wit and beauty are subject to a variant of Gresham's Law which converts them into cliché. The image of red-haired Maggie Smith in a not-great film based on the inadequate stage version of Miss Jean Brodie occludes the wonderful sharpness of Spark's novel (in which Miss Jean is darkly Italianate in looks) and too many people remember MacCaig as a man who wrote funny verse about frogs, not beautiful poems about a man's position in human and natural worlds. Such embourgeoisement exacts from every new generation of genuine writers the task of extracting a certain amount of urine from a complacent literary establishment content with the consensus which it thinks it has achieved. Guns must be fired in defence of wit, beauty and technique.

When I first got to know Edinburgh in the 1960s, after my parents had acquired a flat at the West End, Scottish literary life was in a trough. New Saltire Review flickered fairly brightly, but briefly. Later, Scottish International arrived and soon left. Meanwhile, one was despondently aware of the cult of Compton Mackenzie. One did not realise that this self-appointed Scotsman had once been an interesting, serious novelist. One's heart sank under the idea of 'Monty', author of Whisky Galore, holding court to bewitched old ladies of both sexes in his New Town residence... The myth of Milne's Bar was under formation, though in fact MacDiarmid, who was purported to haunt the place, lived in Biggar and was rarely in Edinburgh, and the unholy trinity of MacCaig, Goodsir Smith and

Garioch, his supporting cast, normally used the Abbotsford. Folkies resorted, of course, to Sandy Bell's, but the significance for literature of what the Prophet Henderson was up to there would only become clear much later...

Looking back, one does indeed perceive that much was disconnectedly happening. Scottish modernisms owing little or nothing to MacDiarmid were emerging in the fiction of Trocchi, Friel and Elspeth Davie while Grieveous inspiration was richly developed and extended in the poetry of Morgan and Crichton Smith. The home rule movement had begun to pick up momentum and this was serving to concentrate the minds of the literati on their potential role in assisting the rebirth of Scotland. Living permanently in Lothian from 1971 on, I was at first preoccupied with helping to raise small children and researching big books. Political news and activity engaged me, the Traverse Theatre could be interesting, but there seemed to be no literary scene to bother about. I first met Joy Hendry on a dreich day in March 1976 or 1977 when she came upon me discussing modern poetry with OU students in a pub after a tutorial, but I couldn't have guessed then how important Chapman, the magazine which she edited and was gallantly hawking, bar to bar, through the rain, would before long become.

That political activity was not enough was starkly revealed by the abortive referendum of 1979. The founding of the Scottish Poetry Library in 1984 involved, very selfconsciously, pre-emptive creation of an institution for a new, autonomous Scotland. During the Culture Wars of the 80s, magazines small in circulation but seeding myriad ideas in media and politics flourished across a spectrum from Radical Scotland, primarily political but interested in literature, through Cencrastus, engaged with philosophy and all the arts disciplines while it published important creative writing, and Chapman, very much part of the home rule movement but most notable for defining a Scottish literary scene in which complete newcomers, later to be famous, were printed side by side with mighty veterans. In the same way, one could organise a poetry reading perming the Grand Old Men – awesome MacLean, sidesplitting MacCaig – with Crichton Smith, Edwin Morgan, Tom Leonard, Liz Lochhead and the very young Jacky Kay to produce an event which one plausibly assumed to be unmatchable in England or any other elsewhere. In the decade when first Alasdair Gray, then Jim Kelman, created new parameters for Scottish fiction and the prophets Nairn and Ascherson performed mind-shifting work for Scottish historico-culturography, one might believe that the arrival of a new short story writer (or painter, or playwright, or composer) was part of the same national movement as produced conferences on the constitution and the famous outbreak of tactical voting in the 1987 election which began the obliteration of the Scottish Conservative and Unionist Party...

The 90s were a decade of constructive cross-party politics which culminated in getting our parliament back, but coincided with an aggrandisement or distortion of literary life by the rise of the cult bestseller. Irvine Welsh, with Rebel Inc desperadoes teeming in his wake, expressed and represented disrespect for all precedents. The success of Trainspotting as book and film was a setback, if not defeat, for 'Scottish literature' as now professed in universities. Welsh claimed to despise not only MacDiarmid but even Trocchi. Battle-scarred footsoldiers of the Culture Wars looked on bemused or aghast. I joked in a piece I wrote nine years back that we

would soon see an Irvine Welsh Heritage Trail.
Blow me, this year's Leith Festival included in
its programme Trainspotting walking tours.
These follow in the wake of the successful
Rebus tours that tracked down Ian Rankin's
bibulous detective to his lair in the Oxford Bar
and coincide with a certain café on George IV
Bridge promoting itself as the 'birthplace of
Harry Potter'. (The cafe in Nicolson Street
where the penniless, lone, lorn Rowling actually
seems to have done more writing is now, sadly
or otherwise, extinct.) Are there McCall Smith
package tours to Botswana? One of many good
things one can say about Iain Banks, who at a
guess probably sells as many books as one or two
just mentioned, is that it's impossible to imagine
such touristification being applied to him.

Pronouncements by metaliterati and politicoes
about 'international recognition' of Edinburgh
as a 'City of Literature' pong strongly of the
solid excrement of male cattle when they recite
the mantra 'Rankin, Rowling, McCall Smith',
sometimes throwing in Welsh as overkill. As it
happens, I find each new Rebus novel in turn
unputdownable, and being an author, I have
to be glad that people are buying books, those
strange little portable rectangular objects,
rather than watching reality TV or incessantly
sending sub-literate texts. But big sales are of
commodities. They are commonly achieved
by deft PR. Even prizes for Booker Men and
Orange Women sometimes have less to do with
wit and beauty than with commodification and
spin. It is hard to see what possible use the 'City
of Literature' tag can have for literature if it
merely provides salaries, junkets and jaunts for
promoters who emphasise its tourism potential,
and salves the consciences of politicians who
are dimly aware that Scottish writers in general
– even some of the best known – are piss-poor,

and dimly imagine that international recognition will somehow pay for these garret-starvers' power cards.

Guerrillas with Guns are needed, hopefully in alliance with Scorpions and our Drouthy neebor, to defy the official reduction of 'literature' to commodity. They should take note of the remark of a friend of mine on hearing that this year's Edinburgh Book Festival will feature 170 Scottish writers: "Good place to have a cull, then." DEATH TO ALL BORES WITH DEGREES IN CREATIVE WRITING should be on our banners, along with CRUSH ALL CLICHÉS and PERSEVERE. Superb writing is being published by small imprints in and around this city. Thirsty Books contributed Peter Burnett's Odium last year and John Aberdein's first novel this. Neither concedes a centimetre to fictional cliché. Helena Nelson has set up a pamphlet imprint, HappenStance, in Fife, to publish her own Unsuitable Poems, which are at least as witty as Dorothy Parker's, and a brilliantly original first collection, Tonguefire, by Andrew Philip. The high-octane performance poet Anita Govan gets her first book out with Luath this autumn. We must hope that James Wood, well known to Gun readers, will get his debut volume out soon. And you should seek out Gavin Bowd's finely crafted poem sequence – 'Hibernaculum' in Markings, issue 19. Wit and beauty have not been smothered yet, though bureaucrats hover with pillows hoping that they will nod off.

Above: Lucy's illustration for A Night At The Highlander (page 131).

Below: Lucy's illustration for the cover of Number 8; whatever the weather, the Editor makes his deliveries.

Last Supper

By James Wood

Patterns written in sheets of glass, lit windows
Form a skin across the ashen lava
That marks this city's outline. Those lights
Bring to mind your eyes, fireflies jabbing
Between the flowers I bought you. Their
    perfume
Lingers at darkness, bringing the strength
To remember past love with kindness.
On my radio
A voice gnaws nervously at the gloom. I
    misunderstand
The signals: unwashed plates, an open book,
    your chair
Pushed away from the table. Empty pans,
    crumbs,
Scraps, crusts of bread. The menacing nightfall,
A half-eaten meal. Those things best left unsaid.

Editor's Introduction: Volume III (2006)

By now firmly established as a leading light in the Capital's grassroots literary scene, we decided on a revamp once again, and the periodical reverted to its original name, albeit with a completely different masthead. Why? Well, I really can't remember the specifics, but I reckon it had something to with ennui and not resting upon our laurels. Our collective boredom thresholds are fairly small after all.

We continued in much the same vein as before, and the pool of writers we could call upon for contributions of quality was very well stocked indeed. We remained as cash-strapped as ever though and as a result put on a few benefit evenings of poetry and song in order to raise a few quid. The success of these evenings led to us to participate in a couple of spoken word-style events, which were great fun, though we did not allow them to distract us from the main agenda.

We began, tentatively, to comment directly on contemporary issues or particular themes, perhaps best exemplified by Lucy's Horgathian illustration for the cover of the first issue of the new volume, which viciously lampooned the last days of sociable smoking in public places.

One of our greatest achievements in Volume III was the first print publication of Alasdair Gray's play Goodbye Jimmy, devoting practically the whole back page to it in order to accommodate yet another classic illustration from Lucy. The first reading of this play was performed at the second run of Thirsty Lunch that autumn, two glorious weeks of free literary performance and much carousing with Angus Calder.

Unfortunately, on a more sombre note, it was at another TL event (which we hosted) that we learned of the death of our dear friend Paul Carter. As noted in my introduction in the issue announcing the tragic and premature news, we are proud to say that Paul contributed more than just words to the Gun.

In the final issue of this volume the use of aliases was finally abolished. From now on, all contributors to the periodical would have to face the public without any masks.

Craig Gibson

Escape From The Royal Ed

A Morningside Adventure

By Craig Gibson

'Twas a beautiful autumnal afternoon, the
kind of Indian summer for which Edinburgh
is famous, and I was sunning myself outside
the inappropriately named Morningside Glory
bar having a few dreamy pints and smoking
like a chimney. I was taking advantage of the
fine weather as I knew that it would soon be
far too cold to imitate the Parisian lifestyle
and that cigarettes would have to be enjoyed
huddled in a doorway or suchlike if one was to
smoke at all while out on the randan. Scores
of schoolchildren from expensive schools were
flocking past me making their way home, much
to my delight, for although I am no pervert, I am
at that stage of my life where I appreciate the
beauty of youth (thanks for that excuse, Oscar).
I noticed rather drowsily amid my reverie that
the Royal Edinburgh Hospital was winking in
the sunlight and I reasoned that it must have
recently received a few licks of white paint.
That'll be nice for them, I thought, for I'd visited
quite a few guests of the Ed over the years,
though thankfully I'd never had any real reason
to join them there on a semi-permanent basis.

Once the kids had all but departed, I decided to
treat myself to a pipe of hash and, as the tables
outside the pub were largely empty, I saw no
harm in smoking it where I was for I prided
myself on my discretion. Big error. On exhaling
my third lungful I became aware of a cop car
sitting at the lights directly in front of me. There
were two of them in the car and the passenger
was staring straight at me with what could only

be described as a look of contempt. Shite. They wasted no time in exiting the vehicle and making a beeline for where I sat.

"What d'ye think ye're playing at?" asked Cop A incredulously. "On yer feet!" He grabbed the pipe from my hands as I complied with his wishes although I remained silent. Cop B proceeded to rifle my pockets, but thankfully I was carrying no ID and less than an eighth in the drug department. This, if anything, made them even angrier. They began to question me and, as I had still refused to say a word, they began to make corny allusions to a night in the cells etc, when I noticed once again, in my peripheral vision, the Royal Ed continuing to wink at me. Suddenly, I had a brainwave which at first seemed absurd, but then many of the best laid plans often are (which is usually why they have a tendency to 'gang aft agley', but we live in hope). I let my head fall forward in the gloomily stereotypical manner I had observed on my visits to the Ed, allowed my jaw to slacken and blurted out in a voice that I hoped sounded thick with Largactil, "Ah'm at the hoaspitul!"

"Eh?" said Cop A.

"Ah'm at the hoaspitul," I repeated even slower than before, and pointed over to the Ed. "Ah'm a schizophrenic. If they ken Ah've been daein the hash again Ah'll get kicked oot an Ah'll be oan the streets an Ah'll no be able tae git ma medication," I continued miserably, hamming it up big style. "Please dinnae tell thum, Ah'm beggin ye!" I rambled on for a bit in this fashion, repeating myself and becoming more and more disorientated. This seemed to genuinely freak them out and they turned away for a brief tête-à-tête. When they turned back to me their manner had changed from aggressive to patronising and

152

they assured me they would not be charging me
with anything, for they did not want to get "the
likes of me" into trouble. I was congratulating
myself on my fine performance and looking
forward to getting the fuck out of Morningside,
when I realised with horror what Cop B had just
said.

"We'd better take you back, Sir, just to make
sure you're safe. We'll keep the pipe and won't
mention the hash, but please be aware that it
is not only illegal, it's twice as dangerous for
someone in your state. We'll just pretend we
found you wandering around confused and
bewildered." And with that he motioned me to
the car and opened the back door.

It is a very short journey from the Glory to the
Ed so I didn't have much in the way of time to
think. I gave the law a bogus name that would
be easy to remember and said little else, rocking
backwards and forwards and groaning softly. All
too soon we arrived through the hospital gates
and I surmised that I was in for some fun and
games at St Leonard's when my deception was
unmasked. My only hope now was to play it
by ear. In the foyer my new chums and I were
greeted by a nurse who, for obvious reasons, did
not recognise me. I acted even more delusional
and stated that I thought I had been admitted
the night before, hoping desperately that the
nurse had only started his shift that morning.
The gods must have decided that I deserved
a bit of good fortune as this was in fact the
case, and he turned away into a small office to
get the admittance records from the previous
night. Taking my cue, I informed the law that
I was about to wet my pants, and could I go to
the toilet please? They suspected nothing and
nodded their acquiescence politely. I was off
down the corridor and as I turned the corner

153

to head left I heard the nurse's voice stating, "There must be some kind of mistake..." I took to my heels with only a few vague memories of the hospital's layout to guide me, and I knew the cops would not be far behind.

Luck was on my side once again for as I sprinted down the corridor I remembered the recreation and smoking room was fast approaching on my right. Peering in through the fug, I recognised a familiar face sitting at the joanna – a long-term patient with whom I had become acquainted on previous visits. He was an old jazz cat, a pianist of no little merit, and he was obsessed with Lee Van Cleef, vampires, Eric Clapton and, somewhat predictably, the Good Book. On my last meeting with this dude he was convinced I was John Lennon (even though, jazz-fashion, he always called you 'Joe' regardless of your name) because I was wearing a fairly Lennonesque hat and wire-rimmed glasses. Well, I was wearing the same hat and glasses combo again and my options were fast running out. I burst into the room, flung open the nearest window and turned to face the jazz man.

"Sammy! Remember me – it's John Lennon! Lee Van Cleef has sent a couple of vampires dressed as cops to kill me! Can you help? Hide me, and when they come tell them I jumped out the window and ran out the back!" I felt slightly guilty lying to him, but I reckoned the truth didn't really matter to old Sam any more and I'd humoured his delusions several times in the past anyway.

"Sure Joe I know who ye are, we've met before, Joe. Hide behind this piano, Joe. If the vampires get ye, Joe, it won't be a holy death like Clapton's son. Quick now, Joe, here they come!"

He was right. I swiftly nipped in behind the piano and crouched down, holding my breath for all I was worth as the door opened. Sammy began to batter out some boogie-woogie and did exactly as I had asked of him.

"He went that way, Joe," he addressed the cops, cackling over the crazy music. "Ye'll need yer wings to catch him!" I could hear them clambering angrily out the window a moment later and I breathed a sigh of relief, emerging from my hiding place and thanking Sam profusely for his kindness. Looking out the window I could see the daft bastards legging it through the garden and into the trees in the opposite direction from the entrance. Sammy tried to give me his Bible as a charm against all vampires, but I refused, telling him he needed it more than me, and after a few Joe-laden pieces of advice I bade him farewell. I too slipped from the window and it was only a short dash to the main gate and freedom. Though sorely tempted by the thought of a stiffener in the Canny's, I didn't fuck around and immediately hailed a taxi on Morningside Road.

Safely ensconced in my Stockbridge local, I mourned the loss of my pipe, for it was a veteran of many campaigns. Still, I reasoned, it could have been a lot worse. The next day I resolved to replace it with a new one and to buy old Sam some Spaghetti Western and Eric Clapton CDs. I would of course have to send them by post and although I didn't know his last name I reckoned that 'Sammy the Jazz Cat, Smoking Room, The Royal Edinburgh Hospital, Morningside' would probably do the trick.

They Wouldn't Accept It Was Over

By Don Birnam

This is the night someone brings a wolf to the
pub. It's docile, lying under the table, until its
great tail cowps its own water bowl and the floor,
already awash with whisky, is made even wetter.

It's the end of a month-long party, and tonight
the bar is full of the kind of people who won't
go home come chucking-out time. Anastasia is
wearing a low-cut black top, a short skirt and
torn fishnets; the punky way she's done her
hair and make-up tempers her usual prettiness.
Natalia's wearing black too, but classy, a cocktail
dress. (We've only known them a couple of
weeks but have spent every night drinking with
them, knowing they'll disappear again soon.
They're performers, and they frequent pubs like
this one; therefore they have a certain kudos
which places them above the average tourist).
They're singing a filthy song, Anastasia playing
the guitar and an old drunk guy managing to
accompany her on the honky-tonk piano. The
song's punctuated by the regular smashing of
whisky glasses, tumbled on to the floor by the
stamping of feet. A coked-up comedian plays a
paper trumpet and Natalia dances, first on the
little tables, then on top of the piano. Nobody
has any idea what time it is; tonight they've made
their own little world of whisky and singing, and
they don't want to know that it's dawn outside.

You know yourself that it's almost entirely an
illusion. This nostalgia you're already feeling so
acutely for something that hasn't yet disappeared
is down to the fact that you're drunk, you tell

yourself, and that for once you have enough money to get another round in. You're creating some kind of miniature golden age in your head, just so that when it's all melted away in the daylight, you can look back and feel sentimental and sorry for yourself. Doesn't it happen every year?

But still, every September, when the empty city wakes up to a giant collective hangover, that lost feeling seems as real as the redundant scraps of posters gathered by the wind and blown with the leaves along North Bridge.

An Edinburgh Vignette

By Andrew Smith

And they danced... oh! How they danced! Soft-
limbed and agile, elegant and supremely joyous,
they moved together as two who would wish
to be one. Pirouette followed arabesque and
strong arms lifted and launched and gave flight
to a delightful leap, graceful beyond measure
and weepingly, achingly, beautiful. They were
twinned together in their art, a will to dance
propelling them to these feats of beauty... oh!
Such beauty! Each move was sublime, flowing
it seemed with such effortless ease, and they
twirled, the maroon red of their jackets billowing
in the evening air. Their charcoal trousers
were loose and allowed the freedom of limb
required for these sumptuous ballets, and the
white cotton of their shirts shone in the glow of
the sodium light. I have seen many dances and
many dancers, many couples, many platforms
upon which such artful magnificence has been
expressed, but it is rare to see two men dance as
these two men did, together. It is rarer still to
see such a dance on a pavement, on Elm Row,
at six-thirty on an Edinburgh autumn evening...
two Lothian Regional Transport bus drivers
dancing together as men possessed in an ecstasy
of heavenly motion.

The Wild Man Of The City

By Kirsti Wishart

It is one of the many fascinating peculiarities
of this city that there is scarcely a vantage point
from which it is possible not to be reminded of
a time before history; a time when the ground
beneath our feet ran molten, giant molluscs
browsed or dragonflies with hang-glider
wingspans flew where pigeons now strut. As too
few of us know, it was James Hutton, the father
of modern geology, who discovered that deep
time and constant motion can turn the bottom of
the sea into the top of hilly peaks and that stone
once poured in rivers along our well-mannered
streets.

It is ironic he developed his theories of geological
flux and instability while walking the familiar
pathways around Holyrood Park in a city that
prides itself on maintaining a certain decorum,
that is reassured by its fixed facade. The danger
today in challenging this rock-solid status quo
can be seen in the reaction to any building which
may disrupt it. Be it a shopping walkway, a
hospital or a Parliament, the guardians against
change and modernity are quick to mock. In
so doing they strengthen in the minds of the
citizenry how this city should look and will look
under their guardianship.

And, by and large, the citizenry are happy to
go along with this, to remain cosseted in a
city which, unlike other cities more vibrant
and dangerous, does not show a different face
every few months. It is only when something
as mundane and terrible as a faulty fuse-box
destroys a large tract of a thoroughfare whose
ugliness seems to be set in law, that passers-by

feel a Huttonesque shiver – the rock beneath your feet can shift, the walls around you melt and possibilities crowd in.

While I certainly do not advocate a similarly dramatic reminder of the forces that can disrupt and unravel our city, leaving opportunity in their wake, I do propose a scheme by which we can be reminded of the precarious nature of our civilised lives. I find it telling that the actor who provides the narration for visitors to Dynamic Earth is John Hannah.

His comforting tones may bring to mind his role as Inspector Rebus, a custodian of our mean streets, one who protects and reassures, keeps us safe from danger. Dynamic Earth, while admirable, does little to instil in its visitors a true sense of shattering awe which may cause them to re-evaluate the insignificance of their office-bound life, throw off the shackles of respectability and start anew; this, I believe should be its true purpose rather than to be an entertaining theme park. While I, restricted by limited funds, do not propose anything grandiose enough to create such a reaction, I do suggest a scheme that will encourage appreciation of how far we have come and how easy it may be to slip through the veil of modernity to a wilder, untamed past.

When Romanticism was at its peak, the aristocracy, to show some sympathy for the aesthetic if not revolutionary demands of that creed, introduced wilder elements into their classical garden arrangements. After a quick visit to the Highlands, they would introduce to their overly genteel estates a newly built tumbledown castle or a small ravine down which a tamed waterfall would trickle. Some would even go as far as to have a bothy-like structure in which a hermit would live in exchange for a few rags and scraps of food on condition that they should emerge and be suitably picturesque when the neighbours visited. I propose a similar individual should be installed in the environs of Holyrood Park, but in order to serve more than aesthetic ends.

At the moment all there is to remind us that Arthur's Seat and Dunsapie Hill were once the homes of Iron Age peoples are the faint remains of their farmland terracing and a tourist information plaque tucked away next to a car-park. A genuine wild man glimpsed stealing pieces of a left-over chicken from a picnic table or gnawing on a fulmar's belly by St Anthony's Chapel would enable visitors to focus their minds more keenly on the ancient past of the site. It may cause them to investigate the flora and fauna of the area further and so gain an appreciation of an area too easily seen simply as a place for a none-too-taxing Sunday jaunt rather than a site of great scientific interest.

Clad in the pelts of rabbits and an unfortunate stray collie, the Wild Man – hired, perhaps, through a government sponsored back-to-work scheme or from QMU's drama department – would remind us of the atavistic responses this bleak landscape of sharp drops and tumbling gorse can produce. He could live in the cave where the famous coffin dolls were found and perhaps ward off potential suicides; they would rather stay at home than face a possible encounter with his rancid breath and roughly-hewn axe. Parents out walking their children and Labradors would keep a sharper look-out and grow more appreciative of their young, while joggers would jog a little faster, slowing their pace only to throw a nervous glance over their shoulder. The pathways named the Innocent

Railway and the Radical Road would gain greater resonance when walkers experienced the thrill of seeing him dart behind a rock and thrilled at the thought of throwing off the responsibilities of conventional lifestyles and returning to a simpler, unfettered time.

There are, I am sure, many who would reject the idea mooted above, perhaps bleating about human rights or public safety or some such nonsense. But for those who have some sympathy, I recommend they reach a point tonight at dusk where they can see the beautiful and dangerous hills of this city and watch as they solidify into an ancient darkness. As you pull your coat tighter against the evening chill, think of a voice not of this time calling out to you, unfettered and fierce. Who among you would be brave enough to answer? And who would slink away to the 'civilised' comforts of potholes, broken street-lights and the letters page of the Evening News?

In Scotland We Know We're Fucked

By Jenny Lindsay

We know we're fucked in January,
That month of long, dreary Sundays,
Where the rain pisses "Good Morning!"
And no-one else fucking does.
The sale signs, gaudy reminders,
That we haven't any money,
It's not the land of milk and honey:
In Scotland we know we're fucked.

We know we're fucked in February,
For, if January's all Sundays,
Then February's Monday morning,
And we have to go to work.
We think life would be better on holiday,
But we can't speak any languages,
And we're suspicious of joviality –
In Scotland we know we're fucked.

We know we're fucked in March,
When we've eaten all the starch,
That is recommended annually,
In order not to die,
Alone, unloved and nobody,
At the tender age of forty,
The thought doesn't dawn on us slowly: .
Naw, in Scotland, we know we're fucked.

We know we're fucked in April,
When we begin to feel unstable,
That four months in we've spent,
Every weekend drunk.
In May a summer beckons,
But June's the wettest month on record,
July brings lots of Americans,
Who think they are not fucked.

We know we're fucked in August,
Especially if we're artists,
Who are not from London,
Or have sponsorship and funds.
For no-one loves a poet,
Who can't be arsed with rhyming,
But that's OK, she knows it:
In Scotland we know we're fucked.

We know we're fucked in September,
When the weather raises its temperature,
Bringing us tender rays of sunshine,
That we watch dismally from our work.
We want our skin to be pink and peeling,
But the general national feeling,
Is of our vitamin D depleting –
In Scotland we know we're fucked.

We know we're fucked in October,
For the year is almost over,
And we still feel bowled over,
By our lack of luck.
We never win the footie,
We're globally known for Connery,
And things we hate like scenery –
In Scotland we know we're fucked.

We know we're fucked in November,
When we start to get a temperature,
And a flu that goes round forever,
So we miss all the fireworks.
But constant bangs and explosions,
Merely lead to harsh abrasions,
And though we haven't been laid in ages,
In Scotland we know we're fucked.

And we're definitely fucked in December,
When we're rocked by violent tempers,
That the year has not yet ended,
So we can make some promises to cheer us up.
It doesn't matter they end up broken,

'Cos we're a proud and brave wee nation,
And we will sing in jubilation,
"In Scoooootland... oh...
Flower of Scotland... when will we see...?"
And then, we'll fall over, fucked.

Measured Mile

By Marc Phillips

The breathy bustling of clean fat people and
sounds of silent reading put him to sleep. Women
digging in their purses and the smell in any
church, these things calm him, just so you know.
Whoever in all hell he is, there's a reason he's
standing here in a scalp-tingling trance, not yet
lost; he's seeking directions.

A well-kempt overweight man of about fifty pulls
away from a wrinkled Morning Messenger to
tell him Bug Shop Road has no sign. It's three
miles past Taw Paw Auto Parts. On the right.
Meanwhile, the lady sitting over there, normal
from the waist up, ass swallowing the secretary's
chair, mines with a badger's intent for a pen,
tampon, or Twix in a Dooney & Bourke knock-off.
This, the only business apparently open on Main,
is the Farm Bureau, Prince Henry County. Oddly,
it seems a place of reverent whispers today, if that.
Essence of oil-soaped pews and musty hymnals
are obviously missing, but not difficult to conjure.

Does the phone even work in here? And, by the
way, "Taw Paw?" Doesn't matter. Don't spell it.
He can't miss it.

He drives over a crosstie bridge spanning Snick
Whim Creek and wonders at what distance the
shot was taken that pierced and creased a small,
square white sign. "Begin Measured Mile." It
was shot – because it was there? No. Because the
shooter was there.

Not a whole lot out here. Ordinary businessmen,
he knows, will sleep spooned-up in shared beds
each night and piggyback to work every morning

for lack of sidewalk space, all the while cursing critical overpopulation in the cities of the world nowadays, long before migrating here. Oh, smile at the stone fissure in that thought. What a thing.

God damn!

Tall Paul's All Parts of the Hog & Produce.

A little blacktop goes off to the right there. He brakes hard – two wheels in the ditch – and bumps a dogwood with his rent-a-Venture minivan making the turn. This tree, should it survive, will become the marker for Bug Shop. Down to the leaning dogwood, take a right, they'll say. Thus, Tall Paul is robbed of this free advertising.

The Venture has impressive acceleration. Indeed, his foot is deep into the rental motor. A cracker on the radio spins a brand of persistent local idolatry in memoriam of Lynyrd Skynyrd's Swampers. And, what's more, there's a grimaced girl with shiny shoes in the road. Frozen there as on a hopscotch grid. Damn her. He brakes hard again.

Her legs thrum on the fiberglass bumper, sounding like a tiny kettledrum. She climbs and flails and molests the wedge of the van like a manic Witch of the East Woods. Skin screeches on the paintjob and windshield. She's a drum-roll on the luggage rack before tumbling off. Does she holler!

There they are, him checking for her pulse in the bar-ditch. In sum, she's burgundy-stained panties peeking from under a bunched summer dress; polished Brogan shoes, likely from the nearest Army-Navy; a girl two years off Tootsie Pops; with titties. Smells like tar and moss out

167

168

here. He's on his knees. There is the muted hum of the Chevy's V6 and not another sound.

"My baby," she moans. It startles him.

"Oh Jesus Christ!"

"Is my baby dead, mister?" She rubs her belly.

"Are you pregnant, honey?"

She sits up, says, "Did it kill it? It killed it, didn't it?"

"Shit! Lie back down. I'll call somebody. Lie back." He grabs for the cell phone on his belt. No service here, though. Not a trickle. "I need to get you to a hospital. I'm going to pick you up."

"Nuh-uh," she says, getting to her haunches. Her dress is tucked into the side of her panties and won't cover her where she needs it.

"Please don't move. You're hurt."

"It aint that bad." She stands, using the top of his head for support. She flinches, her left knee a wobbling skin melon. "Reckon it did the trick though. Ouch!" she hisses, and looks over the van's hood to locate her bag hanging from a low limb of the peeling sycamore across the road. "Am I bleeding fresh? Down there?"

"What?" he asks, still kneeling, holding on to her hips, wishing she won't fall.

"Well you're looking right at it, aint you?"

"I'm looking at your feet, honey. Let me take you to a doctor."

"They're fine, huh? Daddy says very few white people and no niggers at all got shoes like these."

She shoves off his brow and limps three steps.

"Please!" He stands.

"Won't be no doctors, mister. I'll take a couple or three hours getting home. I'll tell 'em a story about what car it was hit me. But they'll be looking for somebody pretty quick."

She falls once, reaching for her bag. He watches, not one thought in his mind, while she rakes among last year's leaves and a green web of briars to find a dead limb, four feet long. Then she is the Wounded Rebel Woman Soldier, worthy of cast concrete monuments in cemeteries, as she props up to shoulder her satchel.

"I have to call somebody," he shouts.

"Is that what you've got to do?" She's struggling away, never turns. "Think on it."

Is this even Bug Shop Road, he wonders? Trees greet one another over the cleared right-of-way in early afternoon doldrums. The blacktop is soft underfoot, some of her hair pushed into it. Not something he wants to be found standing over. Tall Paul's is back that way a quarter mile. The interstate an hour from there.

Son. Of. A. Bitch.

There's something sensual in what just happened, right? Not only secret; also seductive. But she needs a bath.

She whimpers somewhere in all those trees, falling again probably. Maybe it's a mocking bird.

AD 1365

By James Wood

Jerusalem is on edge. The Saracen make ready
To attack God's castle –
Even the bravest men, blood-weary,
Fear this battle.

Their wives and children wait
Impotently
For them to return from war, for Christ
And his Trinity.

God will not stop them: they do not
Believe in Jesus –
All they want is victory
And their share of riches.

They trade in faith and blood,
Shield and sword:
Fine coin and cloth are understood
Better than the Word.

Smoke rises from below. The shouts
Of Allahu Akhbar
Mingle with the scent of corpses
Rotting under the stars.

Time flashes like steel. They stand
Fearing the attack – now
They are challenged, the fiend has risen
And there is no turning back.

The Uneatable In Pursuit Of The Unspeakable

By Michael Conway

At the height of the controversy over the hunting ban, under the headline 'Yesterday, our nation spoke from the heart', William Rees-Mogg ruminated in the Times on his love of country pursuits, particularly '...ferreting, which is the only field sport I have ever practised myself, to catch rabbits during the war.'

Now far be it from me to gainsay a fellow country boy, particularly since he was doing his bit against Hitler and a rather more efficient axis of evil than that which we deal with today. But ferreting?

In case you didn't know, ferreting is a rather basic form of hunting. A sort of semi-tamed polecat is placed into a rabbit warren, and when the frightened bunnies burst out at an enormous lick, they are snared by a wire noose, or caught in a purse trap. It is not a pretty sight. Sometimes the rabbits' heads pop off. Sometimes not. Yet they are very definitely dead, and fit for the pot, with none of those troublesome pellets, the lead ones which have for years added to the marked eccentricity notable among our closely-knit landed gentry.

Still, it's hardly a sport, unlike some of the rural games we got up to in my Galloway youth – an area so countrified we had to hitchhike over sixty miles to Ayr or Dumfries, the nearest towns with populations of more than two thousand, just for amusement.

City people sometimes think life in such places

is an idyll. And maybe it is. But as Conan Doyle observed, through Sherlock Holmes: 'The lowest and vilest alleys of London do not present a more dreadful record of sin than does the smiling and beautiful countryside.'

Indeed, I recently spoke to the mother of an old school friend, from a very douce family, and complained that city children today could never enjoy the freedom we had, prompting her to splurt out in the pure tones of the grande dame: "Yes, Michael, we didn't know what you all were up to – and we didn't want to."

Absolutely. Even today I quake with fear at the very thought. Yet, they, too, bear some of the responsibility, since from the age of three we were kicked out the door, and if we came back without a bloody nose or a bloody knee, or at least being well covered in muck, parental looks suggested something had gone seriously astray.

And what did we get up to in that idyll, the Machars of Wigtownshire? I observed (but did not necessarily take part in) the following country pursuits: spearing rats at the town dump with sharpened bows and arrows; air-rifling any birds which came to hand; forcing crabs at the Quay to fight (named Crabiatores, after one of the first books of the Cambridge Latin Course, Gladiatores); running after woodlice with magnifying glasses at the height of summer, and setting up the bonfires of other boys the night before Guy Fawkes with siphoned petrol. In between times, scrumping apples at the Red Gates, Croft-an-Righ and, most excitingly, the 'old teacher with the dogs' place'. Making bangs with a mix of weed killer and ground-up battery was another favourite; soldering it into metal tubes, and blowing the result up at the disused aerodrome; and, after running out of weed killer,

fabricating gunpowder out of ancient relatives'
constipation medicine (sulphur), butchers'
preservative (saltpetre), and the ever-useful
ground up battery (carbon).

The gunpowder proved to be not half so much
fun as the weedkiller, though activities were put
on hold when the local chemist, er, pharmacist,
overheard plotting about the correct proportions
for a really good bang – the conspirators were
poring over the Encyclopaedia Britannica, while
he lurked behind the cowboy section of the
library – and then stopped abruptly the supply of
flowers of sulphur (a late grandfather's favourite
laxative), at the next asking.

Despite all this, nothing much happened to us.
We didn't shoot hands or legs or fingers off with
our air rifles, as our parents had done with their
parents' shotguns – in fact we shot nothing much
at all, since accurate marksmanship is a life-long
learned skill. The rats and woodlice were far
more clever than their persecutors. The crabs
never fought, since they were all female, the only
ones to come on shore. Occasionally, the other
boys set up our bonfire. Even the apples we
pinched, pinched us, since they were small and
immature, and even the relatively strong sun in
this southernmost part of Scotland – they grow
palm trees on the Rhinns peninsula – cannot
ripen the unripenable. Our stomachs ached for
weeks.

Still stomach-aches recede, yet morally
conscientious aches remain. What about John
Ballantyne (not his real name) – a teenager
who died of true, rural poverty – of the kind
described forty years before by the late Ian Niall,
in his book Wigtown Ploughman (1939), which
caused such a storm it forced governmental
action – killed by asphyxiation and fire, along

with three of his younger cousins, attempting to heat his parentless home with cut-up bits of tyre?

Every small community has a family like the Ballantynes, reminiscent of the untameable Connollys in Evelyn Waugh's Put Out More Flags (1942). Large, ill-educated, rough, and very useful. They are blamed for everything, and the police are always at the door. 'The usual suspects', as it were, a paradigm of racism in an all-white community.

The story is this. A hole had been discovered in the outhouse which served as a local hostelry's cellar. Unmuscular youngsters could with some difficulty sneak through and steal a few tins of the then fashionable drink, Breaker Malt Liquor. It was dead easy, even in the October darkening. Until, that is, it appeared through the unlit gloom that a local woman of influence – the seamstress – had espied the trio in the very act. Six months later, and some few weeks before his tragic death, John Ballantyne was sentenced to nothing much in Stranraer Sheriff Court for said activity. Whether he was actually guilty, or whether discovering the same opening he came to the same childish and mildly criminal conclusion, or whether he was completely innocent and 'fitted up' to fill a police clear-up report, is immaterial. This much is true. The other culprits, had they been caught, would have received at most an admonishment (or warning) from the procurator fiscal. Instead, but for the disaster with the Firestone radials, Ballantyne had already started on the process which would have led him inexorably on the road which finishes either in Barlinnie or in heroin-assisted death (non-traditional drugs had not yet been invented, at least in this part of the world, but they soon would infect even the most rural areas).

The equally culpable trio had parents with some influence, and apart from the high jinks of adolescence, were each doing well at school. Hugh MacDiarmid's description of the Scottish mindset as a 'Caledonian antisyzygy' – the sort of aspect of character which allowed Lord Cockburn to be a judge one minute and the raffish 'Cocky' the next, or persuaded Stevenson to create Dr Jekyll and Mr Hyde out of the pitiable story of Deacon Brodie, Edinburgh councillor by day and thief by night, who was hanged on a gallows of his own devising – was all too true in their case. One now holds the Queen's Commission. Another is currently building Kuala Lumpur. And the last – the lookout, who imagined he saw the seamstress over the garden wall – is...

Ah, country sports? You can't beat 'em. So character forming.

Pettypip

By Angus Calder

Bereft of expectations
I went east
where I learnt from small Bengalis
the art of making curries
with tiny touches of spice.
I implore you not to hurl in
six chillies, ten cloves of garlic,
tablespoonfuls of tamarind
and turmeric.
Be silversmith not blacksmith.
Know your onions, friend:
not too many. Well-washed rice,
burly river fish –
ingredients should be simple.
Intelligent attentiveness
creates the feast
you wish.

Above: The end of an era and the introduction of
the smoking ban, as depicted by Lucy McKenzie
on the cover of Number 9.

Below: Lucy observes the Gun High Command at
work on the cover of Number 12.

Dark Seagull

By Angus Calder

Passing Bruntsfield Links, paradisal arena of her
girlhood, in blustery April sunshine, just after
news of the death of Muriel Spark, it pleased me
to fancy that she was still among us, her soul
having taken the form of a soaring seagull. The
image won't now go away, but it's not quite right.
Leaving aside the fact that Catholic Spark would
have recoiled from the idea of metempsychosis, a
single seagull, though lovely, is far from unique,
whereas Spark was an extraordinary one-off.

She was a writer from the very small ethnic
minority of Edinburgh Jews, and egregious even
in this instance because while her father was
straight Jewish, her mother's father was a Jew
who had married a southern English Anglican.
One is Jewish by descent through one's mother,
so technically Muriel Camberg wasn't Jewish.
The religion of her beloved James Gillespie's
school by the Links was relaxed Church of
Scotland. In London later, she worshipped as
an Anglican then, in her late thirties, without
'blinding revelation', but through slowly
accumulated intellectual conviction, she was
received into the Roman Catholic Church.

Her literary development was not much less
zigzag. As a twelve-year-old, she was already
acknowledged bardess of Gillespie's, with a
batch of five poems accepted for a young people's
anthology. Poetry was her medium until in her
thirties she suddenly won the major Observer
short story competition. It was years before she
made much money from fiction but the success
of The Prime Of Miss Jean Brodie (1961), in
print, adapted for Broadway and the West End,

and as Oscarised movie, gave her the freedom to live as and where she chose. She chose to revisit Scotland rather rarely.

She had abandoned secretarial work in Edinburgh, aged 19, in 1937, to travel to Rhodesia to marry a teacher named S O Spark – SOS, geddit? He was a neurotic fruitcake, the marriage swiftly failed, but because of wartime travel restrictions it was 1944 before she struggled back to Britain, minus her little son. After a spell as a black propagandist in the notorious Bletchley équipe, she settled in London, with a succession of ill-paid journalistic and editorial jobs. Success as a novelist temporarily lured her to New York, then permanently to Italy.

The geographical range of her fiction was accordingly large. She achieved international recognition, and so she should've. The superlatives which flooded the press after her death were justified. Her prose, while more exuberant than Jane Austen's, was equally deadly in its wit. She could match her admirer Evelyn Waugh in the generation of bizarre yet somehow credible characters, and her theological musings were as interesting as those of another admirer, Graham Greene, and perhaps more subtly transmitted. It is a moot point whether Brodie – brief enough to see first publication in its entirety in a single issue of the New Yorker – is a novella or a short novel. I think the latter, but it is more significant that in her deftness of construction, Spark equalled the great master of long-short fiction, Ivan Turgenev. She herself connected her originality of method to her conviction that "the novel as an art form was essentially a variation of a poem". She always thought of herself "predominantly as a poet".

To return to the Links... They were on her
way from her home in Bruntsfield Place to
Gillespie's, on the edge of Marchmont. "I
loved crossing the Links to school in the early
morning, especially when snow had fallen
in the night or was still falling. I walked in
the virgin snow making the first footprints of
the day... I loved the Bruntsfield Links in all
seasons." She also loved her school, where her
precociousness was not underrated and most of
the teachers were pleasant and useful people.
As for Bruntsfield itself (which she thought
of as part of Morningside) she revelled in the
variety of its shops, its characters, its peculiarly
Edinburgh kind of friendliness. Well over half of
Curriculum Vitae, her memoirs of her first four
decades, published in 1992, was devoted to warm
memories of Edinburgh – flecked, of course, with
pathos, and inset with a diversion to holidays in
her mother's Watford. The vividness of detailed
recall is delightful.

She does not ignore the downside of inter-
war Edinburgh, with mass unemployment
and with poverty snapping at the heels of the
genteel Cambergs. Edinburgh snobbery is not
underestimated. But overall the city is made
to seem radiantly delightful. The remaining
two-fifths or so of Spark's book takes us from
paradise into hell and purgatory...

Beautiful though parts of Rhodesia are, the
racism and pettiness of its white settlers were
disgusting. Black propaganda – telling lies to the
Germans – spawned odd human relationships,
notably with the German POWs selected to
broadcast to their folk back home. As editor of
the Poetry Society's Poetry Review in the late
forties, Spark fell foul of the absurdly reactionary
tastes of committee members and the outraged
vanity of bad poets. Her long-term lover and

collaborator in the fifties, Derek Stanford, turned
out to be a mediocre poet, and a bad scholar,
personally treacherous. Spark battled against
poverty and malnutrition and went through a
phase of madness. Her son meanwhile grew up
apart, with her parents in Edinburgh.

Though there are important Scottish elements
in The Ballad Of Peckham Rye (1960) and
Symposium (1990), Brodie (1961) is Spark's
only novel set entirely in Scotland. But I don't
think it is just local prejudice on our own part
if we use it as a key to her entire oeuvre and to
her uniquely Sparkish way of seeing things. I
think that it's the book in which she introduces
conditions and phenomena of purgatory and hell
into her paradisal childhood wonderland: beauty
and vileness, disgust and rapture, comedy and
tragedy come together.

No one doubts that Miss Christina Kay at
Gillespie's was the original of Miss Brodie – the
charismatic, unorthodox teacher who takes
chosen pupils to ballet and plays, talks about
paintings, expands their artistic sensibilities.
But whereas Miss Jean is vain, shallow, fascistic
and dangerous, Spark's memories of Miss Kay
are entirely positive. Nor does she recall a
rampant Knoxian spirit dominating Gillespie's
such as, in her novel, centres at Marcia Blaine's
on headmistress Mackay. The dishy Gillespie's
art master Cooling was a bit of a lad as Spark
recalls him, but not a precedent for his one-
armed, almost perverted counterpart at Marcia
Blaine's. And so on...

There are patches of lyrical writing in Brodie,
but the influence of Robert Louis Stevenson
on Spark – admittedly enormous – helps her
provide the image of a city psychologically flawed
from top to bottom. Another cardinal influence

were the Border ballads, with their flashes of sudden violence and their matter-of-factness about doom and destruction. They provide one precedent for Spark's supremely economical narrative method, which exposes by contrast the redundancies of explanation offered by lesser writers.

The thousands who flock to any theatre in Edinburgh which puts on the rather disappointing stage adaptation (not by Spark herself) of Brodie, and the millions who have enjoyed the not-bad movie based on it, miss the subtlety and poise of Spark's presentation of Brodie on the page. She is and she is not evil. Sandy Stranger's betrayal of her is and is not forgivable. The city of light is a maze of dark places.

It is right to point out in conclusion that Ian Rankin, whose Rebus novels have provided a near-comprehensive social and moral geography of Edinburgh and its dark places, diverted into writing fiction himself from postgraduate study of Muriel Spark (and, like her, bears the mark of RLS). The seagull over Bruntsfield Links in another light could be the crow which before Duncan's murder in Macbeth 'takes flight for the rooky wood'.

God Saved The Class of '85

By Rodge Glass

At 10.12am on 14 June 1985, a small explosion
went off in the kitchen of Saint Andrew's
Academy in Edinburgh while seventeen students
sat their Higher maths exam in the canteen next
door. These seventeen comprised those with
surnames starting with the letters T to Z; A to S
took the test on the other side of the premises,
nearly a quarter of a mile away – Saint Andrew's
Academy was the largest in the city, and was well
known for it. The headmistress used to say (with
tiresome regularity) that Jesus Christ himself
could visit the chemistry block at first period and
news might not reach modern languages before
the end of the day. She had a point. Nobody
told students A to S of the events of 14 June until
they had safely finished adding, subtracting,
multiplying and dividing their way through the
exam – pens down, arms folded, papers clearly
labelled with their names. In the aftermath,
they would all be offered counselling anyway.
The headmistress was the soft sort who thought
teenagers needed to be cuddled into responsible
behaviour. I do not agree with that claptrap.

The kitchen staff of Saint Andrew's had recently
employed a nervous young cook who was so
anxious to please superiors that her hands shook
continually while on the job. Her first task each
morning was to turn on the gas flame on one
of the main hobs, but, fingers trembling, on 14
June she lit the match and dropped it on to her
uniform, which quickly caught fire. Before she
was able to put herself safely out, she slipped and
cracked her head on a sideboard – the poor girl
began to burn, unconscious – and when the head
cook found her aflame she screamed, flinging her

184

heavy arms out to her sides, thumping a large
container of oil onto the floor, her colleague, and
herself. The whole kitchen went rapidly red, and
BANG! If any member of the local health and
safety board could have seen the mess of coats,
bags, paper and plastic littering the kitchen
hallway that helped the fire along that day in
Edinburgh, they would have been appalled.
Kitchen staff would not get away with that kind
of recklessness in these litigation-conscious
times. The papers would create an almighty fuss.
But, those days weren't these, and what wouldn't
be there now was certainly there then – so why
dwell? The racing heat made its way fast from
the kitchen out towards the rest of the school,
starting with the canteen.

Back in the exam room, one child, Thomas
Tate, whose father was a fire-fighter, was ideally
positioned to see what was coming, being the
first alphabetically and seated closest to the
blaze. He reacted quickly and ordered all the
other students into an adjacent room; knowing
his background, they obeyed. Thomas closed
the door and set about battling the fire with the
help of a fire extinguisher – when it ran dry he
retreated into an adjacent room with the other
students, blocking the gap under the doors with
blankets usually used to cover canteen tables.
This, as anyone with experience of these sorts of
things knows, prevented smoke getting through
to the students who all huddled in this storage
cupboard where, among other things, matches
were kept. Which is a frightening thought,
really.

Thomas prayed for the wail of his father's
engine, fully expecting the fire to burn through
the door and melt him and his friends one
by one. But no, the fire raged outside only,
seeming shy of intruding on the crammed space.

Thomas later gained so much respect among his peers for his bravery that he decided to join the family business when he grew up: which he did. But on that day in 1985 he was already a hero. Meanwhile, on the other side of the blaze, members of the kitchen staff panicked. They did not think to call the emergency services immediately, which was why Thomas and friends were trapped for nearly fifty minutes before fire engines came to set them free.

After paying tribute to the lost cooks and his colleagues' bravery, the fire chief said it was a miracle that none of the students had perished as well; surrounded by local and national television crews, representatives of the press, parents, relatives, friends, and some local residents, the fire chief concluded his brief report, then handed over to the headmistress, who answered queries. Some of these were angry ones; people felt swindled out of information. "Surely one boy could not have held back a fire for so long?" they asked. "Will the students be allowed to retake their exams?" "Why did no alarms go off?" "How did the fire start?" "You're a bloody liar!" one parent cried out from the back. "This story doesn't add up, does it?" To which the headmistress gave sensible, dull answers that sounded perfectly plausible but meant little. She was then asked the question: "How is it possible that these young people are still alive?" The headmistress clasped her hands and said in a low, slow, solemn voice: "There is no other explanation. God saved the class of '85". Well! Snap snap snap, and that was the image on the front of the newspapers the following day: the headline had already been written.

Above, from top: Lucy McKenzie's portraits of
Craig Gibson, Gerry Hillman and herself, from
Number 12.

The Hebrew Word For Fuck

By Peter Burnett

ענה

You don't read Hebrew, but that's not a problem.
In a matter of minutes you'll be fluent. You'll
have grasped the weirdness and duplicity of the
ancient language and been introduced to two of
its slipperiest words. Like all Biblical languages,
Hebrew doesn't translate well into modern
English. It's the issue of vocabulary – not ours,
but theirs. There's no word for television because
there was no such thing in the Bible – dummy!
– just as there's no word for rape – there being no
rape in the Bible.

Printed above is the word that is never translated
as rape. You can pronounce it ahnaah. This is
a word with a dozen connotations. It means to
oppress or upset, or even to depress someone,
as in Psalm 88: "Thou has depressed me with all
thy waves." It is the genius of this language, that
correctly expressed, this same word can mean rape.

No one was raped in ancient times, you see.
There is no such word as rape in the Bible because
there is no conception of such a thing. Our idea of
rape assumes that a woman possesses the right to
determine her own sexual partners. In the Bible,
when a woman is raped, it is typically her father's
or husband's rights that are violated – not hers.
This is why the crime of rape is expressed with
the above Hebrew word, a word which refers to
humiliation.

"Do not humiliate me!" pleads Tamar when her
half-brother Amnon overpowers her. (It's all in 2
Samuel 13. Ask the minister).

188

In Judges chapter 19, an innocent concubine is gang fucked to death by a mob of Biblical perverts, an act which, believe me, receives scant attention in the theological colleges and Torah schools of the world. The act is referred to as the woman's being used, which is something of a euphemism given that the devirgination goes on until dawn.

שׁגל

Fuck. You can pronounce it shagahll – to sound like the name of the Russian-born French painter. My own prudish Hebrew dictionary offers the English translation of shagahll as "to be rutty" – but it means something much worse than that. In fact, the word shagahll was so disturbing to Israel that when the Masoretes rendered the Bible official, somewhere between the 6th and 10th centuries, they deleted it – but it is in fact the Hebrew word for fuck. Deuteronomy uses God's own words to express what will happen to Israel if it fails to keep its covenant. "You will become engaged to a woman and another man will fuck her." That was straight from the Old Boy's mouth and you can't say fairer that that.

Isaiah's 13th chapter is a prophecy against Babylon, in which the prophet delights in the fact that Babylon's wives will be fucked – and Zechariah Chapter 14 is another typical threat from God – "I'll gather all the nations," says God, "and send them to fuck the women of Jerusalem."

Where is this taking us? I just thought you'd like to know before the sermon begins, that the Old Testament cannot bring itself to use the most violent word it knows (fuck) to apply to rape. It must be a comfort to religions, that when the raping begins in earnest, it's only a matter of the boys twatting the odd expendable whore in an act that is referred to – at the very best – as humiliation. Why would the good old boys of the good old book (and God for that matter) wish to defile themselves with unpleasant notions such as rape?

The answer is that they wouldn't. To them, nothing is more important than your good faith. There are 400 rapes half way through Judges Chapter 21 – and another 400 at the end. I'm not allowed to call these rapes rapes, however – although presumably I'm allowed to meditate on them when I'm praying. Presumably, it's not rape if it's sanctioned from above. Presumably, there is a moral. If there is, I think it must be that only God is allowed to fuck.

I'm Being Followed

By Don Birnam

I've got something to tell you
I've got something to tell you
I'm being followed
I'm being followed

I'm being followed by Alexander McCall Smith

He followed me here and he'll follow me home
(Or would, if I lived in the New Town)
He'll be lurking in Dundas Street, waiting
With a philosophical digression at the ready
He'll write me, thinly disguised, into tomorrow's
    Scotsman
(He's got most of my friends already)
He won't let me rest, he's completely obsessed,
He's turning me into an Edinburgh type!

I'm being followed by Alexander McCall Smith

And it doesn't stop there
Inspector Rebus moved in next door
I moved house – but that Rankin's too clever
He transferred his detective to Gayfield Square
So I'm still on his beat
There's no escape
There's no escape when you're being followed by
    a fictional policeman

So you won't catch me in the Cumberland these
    days
I don't go near the Oxford Bar
Leith is out of bounds
(I don't like the way Irvine Welsh has been
    looking at me)
In fact you won't catch me out much at all
I don't go out much any more
I mostly just stay in and read...

Above: Lucy McKenzie's imagining of the set
and properties for Alasdair Gray's play Goodbye
Jimmy, from Number 10.

The Smoke Museum

By Kirsti Wishart

There are some today who refuse to believe in the
Smoke Museum. They prefer to think it a story
dreamt up by disgruntled smokers and this is
understandable. Shut to the general public for
years, the Smoke Museum is hidden in an area
of a city rarely visited. The ornate three-storey
building could not be tolerated in healthier times
and there are citizens who would be outraged to
discover it had not been demolished decades ago.
They would be surprised to learn the museum
was shut without ceremony, but not without
protest, after the death of its founder, and yet it
remains open to a select few, continuing to stand
as a memorial to less enlightened times and a
monument to one remarkable man.

The Smoke Museum was the creation of one of
the city's leading tobacconists. He was also a
philanthropist, hardly a year going by without
him setting up some new bequest or award, a
library here, a swimming pool or art gallery there.
The Smoke Museum was to be his crowning
achievement in a life of tobacco, a celebration of
his one vice in life. He was a respectable man,
pillar of the community, married to Edith for 35
years, father to five children. The only thing that
held his interest, other than the business and
family responsibilities, was tobacco. A museum
would help sell his products, of course, but it
would be a memorial to the one clear memory of
his father, who died at sea, swept overboard from
a tobacco ship when William was ten. Sitting in
the armchair always kept free for him during his
long voyages at sea, he would watch proudly as
William, perched on the arm beside him, puffed
on a cigarette brought all the way from Tanzania.

The tone of pride in his voice, when William
inhaled deeply and blew out the blue-tinged
smoke without choking. "See, Edith? A real son
of mine," tapping him on the shoulder, the only
touch from the man he can remember.

After his father's death, William Webb held
cigarettes, cigars, cheroots, pipes, even hookahs
in fascination. They suggested a rich bohemian
underworld and, as soon as he earned his first
pay-packet as a paperboy, he began collecting.
His books of cigarette cards from around the
world filled several shelves in his private library.
There were many cigarette packet designers
who would have wept with joy if they could be
granted a glimpse of the prototype sketches he
had acquired for famous packet designs. A quiet
man, he was at his most talkative when speaking
to his foreign agents who travelled the world
investigating the smoking habits of other regions
on the Webb Company's behalf. He would listen
with a childlike wonder to stories of hookah
use in Turkish harems, the preferred brand of
cigarette papers used by Russian intellectuals
and of the various ways African tribes treated a
particular type of bark to make it smokable.

In the month leading up to the day of the
grand opening of the Smoke Museum, a former

cigarette-rolling factory, the city talked of little else. Small crowds would gather outside the building, speculating on what the mysterious boxes and crates could contain, what was hidden by the drapes on either side of the entranceway. On the day itself, the answer was revealed as two large mechanical Russian soldiers, rings of light blue smoke appearing from their busby-like helmets. Webb himself took great pride in cutting the opening ribbon commenting only to the assembled journalists that he was very pleased to see this day arrive. If the Museum gave the citizens half as much pleasure as he gained from tobacco he could retire a happy man; this the longest recorded speech he had ever granted the press. Webb's Finely Blended Cigars were handed out to the men, Webb's Lights to the ladies, along with warnings that smoking was strictly prohibited within the Museum. The risk of fire and the destruction of valuable, irreplaceable objects was too great.

Maps were provided in the grand foyer as it was easy to become lost in the exhibition spaces, formerly offices, of the upper levels. The hall, which had previously housed long tables seating hundreds of expert rollers, was the central exhibition space. The rolling tables had been replaced with display case after display case, filled with various items from Webb's own collection along with artefacts his commissioned team of anthropologists, explorers, designers and salesmen had sought out for him. The pick of his cigarette card collection filled several. Matchboxes, crafted with incredible skill, were in another and guides could provide spectators with magnifying glasses so the viewer could appreciate the beauty and intricacy of the small panels; a view of Japanese pagodas with each petal of cherry blossom minutely detailed, two bluebirds flying above and Mount Fuji in the background; Seurat's The Bathers; a country house, with a garden in full bloom and shadowy intrigues dimly visible through its many windows. Cigarette papers used by spies in the course of their secret missions were on show. Scribbled codes and ciphers were translated along with accounts of whether the agents had lived or perished while securing the country's safety. The lighters of famous city gangsters, one showing the mark of the bullet that should have killed Shorty McClue, were there on loan from the police department.

In the other rooms on the upper levels, the exhibits were considered more risqué and, some would say, even more entertaining. One housed several elaborately jewelled Turkish and Persian hookahs, one of which was smoked by an authentic Islamic holy man, roped off from the crowds and seated or recumbent on large Oriental-style cushions. Occasionally he was replaced by a woman, described by the newspapers as a dusky maiden, whose harem-style pyjamas scandalised many, as did her habit of winking lazily at members of her audience. This room led on to the cigarette-testing machine, its bellows working at a contraption made of iron, rubber and silk designed to simulate the motion of a smoking human being, its puckered 'lips' constantly replenished with cigarettes by a member of staff. When a few switches were flicked the machine could produce smoke rings, a love heart, or a five-pointed star.

The first reviews and articles were sceptical of the museum. They rejected the idea it was a source of education, pointing out the absence of any reference to slavery or the gathering of tobacco. They called it Webb's Folly, said that it was a waste of time and money to celebrate so ephemeral a pleasure and foretold its closure within a few months. However, these journalists reckoned without the appeal the attraction held for the general public. Crowds thronged and gained tremendous satisfaction from examining a product they could buy from their local tobacconists and slip into their pocket, here seeing it treated as a work of art. The Smoke Museum collection grew as citizens brought in mementos they felt would be better looked after by the curators than themselves.

William Webb continued to take a great interest in the museum, visiting it after a long day in the office once the crowds had left, checking visitor numbers and takings and viewing any new exhibits. Over the years his visits became more frequent as he began to hand control of his business interests over to his children. Ironically, as the money the Webbs made increased, the number of philanthropic gestures declined. Thomas, his eldest son, argued that when a company gets bigger more money has to be spent on keeping it maintained. His father, trusting Tom's judgment, concurred but made sure there was still enough money to keep the museum going. There was always something new to add, whether it be a form of pipe used by a recently discovered tribe from Papua New Guinea or the donation on the death of a Finnish collector of matchboxes from around the world. Somehow space was always found and when the space ran out, he bought the disused warehouse next door and began filling that.

Then came the double blow. The scandalous behaviour of the youngest Webb, Jack resulted in him leaving the city in disgrace. Edith, after having retreated to her private rooms, refusing to speak to anyone, died of a broken heart. In the years that followed William withdrew completely from business life but maintained his obsession with the museum. Indeed, it reached the point where he was rarely in residence at the Webb mansion but instead had a room fitted out in the museum itself with a bed, washstand and small gas stove. Guards spoke of seeing him pace the corridors at night, chuckling over his favourite exhibits as if seeing them for the first time.

As the fortunes of the Webbs took a downturn, the atmosphere of the museum began to change. Eccentric philosophies began to undermine its educational aspects. Joseph Cresswell, the critic, wrote of visiting the museum and revelling in the opportunity to enjoy the ephemeral nature of the perfect cigarette, the way in which the habit of smoking enables the smoker to enjoy moments outside the daily run of events. He drew attention not only to the beauty of the image hung in the foyer of a sunflower made from the silver and gold inner foil of hundreds of packets donated by visitors but also to how fragile it was, how easy it would be to destroy. The museum became one of the main meeting points for the city's existentialists, who would walk the rooms with wry, world-weary amusement. Odd rituals began to take place in alleyways running either side of it. People would come and burn photographs, letters, mementos they wanted to be free of. Drawings and insane writings on the 'true' message of cigarette packets were found shoved down the back of the display cabinets.

Eventually the museum fell victim to wider changes taking place in the city. Family and friends of those who had died through suspected smoking related illnesses began to picket the museum's entrance. As a concession, a few health warnings were added to displays, a room tucked away next to the exit showed blackened lungs and stunted babies, but the film usually played to an empty space. Those who did watch only did so to heighten the delicious sense of transgression exuded by the other exhibits. A room promoting the various health claims made for cigarettes, pipes and cigars was at the very top of the building. It became difficult to appreciate the assurances that smoking Cherries Own Blend could help prevent a cold, or that it was better to reach for a Slimstar instead of a chocolate, when surrounded by the wheezing and hacking of life-long devotees of the product being celebrated. The crowds dwindled the opposition grew.

Finally one morning a guard, who was in the habit of bringing Webb his daily paper when he stayed overnight at the museum, tapped on the door to no response. Smelling gas and a strange charring, he opened the door and saw the gas stove burning harmlessly and Webb, sitting in the chair, his left arm resting on a table next to it where photographs of his family sat. His hand held a portrait of Jack, always his favourite. The right arm was draped down over the other side of the chair, a black cheroot scorching his unfeeling fingers.

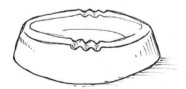

Flowers

By Reggie Chamberlain-King

Returning home after a long, hard having-a-
hard-time-of-it, I pass beneath the road via the
subway-walk – where there are some graffito-
savvy kiddos. About as young as a dog in dog
years, hair cut back to nought by clippers,
T-shirts sporting logos like 'massacre', 'poverty'
and 'embarrassment'. Balls in aerosols crack
back and forth as each shakes a can vigorously.

As I, a man and adult, approach, they do not hide
these instruments of destruction behind their
backs. Rather, I am approached as well; the cans
are held forward in their hands.

"You don't mind, do ya mister?" ask the
delightful, puppy-fat-faced cherubs.

"Not so long as you spray something pretty,"
replies the dashing hero, me.

"Would some flowers do?"

"Yes, indeed, young fellow. Some flowers are
very pretty indeed." I, the hero, let them be, but
not without playfully clipping their ears, as a
fancier would a pigeon's wings...

*

... I check back later, in the hope that some
fanciful artwork of peonies and posies was
now under the boardwalk, faux-tosynthesising
in the darkness. But not a flowering bud, in
sight, in that subway, was there, seen by my
eyes and no, nor any others. Not even a fresh
batch of children's nomenclature (Mick, Titch,

Dozy, Dee etc etc). I ascended the stairs a little disappointed that the bairns had not taken the way of the aesthete, but, overall, glad that the grubby subway walls were no more besmirched with the words of the prophet or childish braggadocio than previously. Coming out into the sunshine, I, the hero and ever the aesthete, went forth to the council's hanging baskets to inhale all the Lord's olfactory pleasures. But not the scent of natural marigolds and carnations met my nose, nor, on unscrunching my eyes, was I was greeted by their natural hue.

The smell was that of just-aerosol-leaked paint and the petals were all a beautiful, dripping blue. It seemed they had picked the way of the aesthete after all.

Editor's Introduction: Volume IV & Number 17 (2007 – 2008)

In keeping with tradition we decided to launch Volume IV with a new masthead and, perhaps more importantly, a new slogan: Wisdom – Industry – Magic. However, as bold as this stance might have appeared, we were in fact getting a little weary after four skint years in the literary trenches. Indeed, we became so battle-fatigued that we found ourselves participating in the 'Art' scene of Edina and, indeed, produced a one-off Gun for a group show in Athens. Whilst this special edition helped to fulfill our self-imposed obligation to produce four issues a year, it is considered by the High Command to be non-canonical (and completely against our ethos – we received cash for producing it and the only copy in the Editor's possession is almost contemptuously stained with wine) and as such is not represented in this anthology – with the exception of James Wood's specially commissioned poem.

Despite this error of judgment, we were still able to produce three fine issues and welcomed yet more writers, poets and cartoonists to the ranks. Nevertheless, due in part to a few fuck-ups in my personal life, the winter edition of Volume IV was to be the last Gun release for over six months.

Doubters and other swine may have wondered, "Is that it?"

Well no, it wasn't and isn't.

2008, mid-summer, and another Gun is loosed upon the public (slogan: Literature For Heroes). We were pragmatic though. Rather than announce a new volume, we decided to break with the norm and simply label the latest issue 'Number 17'. I had long had a problem with the shite notion of the Capital's so-called 'duality' and so had issued a communiqué to our core of writers beseeching them to help venomously disparage this crap once and for all. The response was excellent.

I am so proud of the (anti) 'Duality' edition. Didn't make us many friends though, ha ha!

Number 17 also contained one of the hardest things I've ever had to write, which was our beloved Angus Calder's obituary. Though we had known he was seriously ill for some time, 'twas still a real blow. The first words in this anthology are rightfully yours, Don Calder. As a tribute to the man we have also included in this volume Angus' tale Upcountry which is previously unpublished.

2008 also witnessed the death of Gun contributor and principal stalwart Barry McLaren, First Duke of Mercury. Dear Baraldo, y'r loyalty will never be forgotten!

Though Number 17 was in many ways the perfect issue, I felt I had finally expended my considerable bile and it seemed to me that the Gun's course had run to its logical conclusion. Had we succeeded in our mission? Well, it depends upon how one regards success, but I reckon we had done what we set out to do; namely provoke, entertain and inspire in equal measure. It was definitely time for a well-earned rest.

The One O'Clock Gun is officially 'asleep' at the time of writing, but like the legendary King Under The Mountain we will awaken again when the time is right. In what guise I do not know, but believe you me, we most certainly WILL be back!

Pax Edina!

Craig Gibson

At Junction Thirteen

By Michael Conway

1

In the pub called Junction Thirteen, Jimmy felt
the aura. He had come here to drink, for heaven's
sake, and so why did he have coffee? At this time
of the year, of all times, indeed. Hadn't he been
warned enough? Don't think about it! Don't. But
it was very heavy, it was pressing, it was going
to happen. He struggled out, depersonalisation
coming over him – his own tell-tale sign – until
he got to the launderette, the launderette where
the opinion pollster always lurked, the place of
warmth, of motherly women, and – pray Jesus!
– safety. The place of gauze and Ariel and
Comfort – the place where he lay down at the side
of the tumble dryer, so as not to fall...

The place where the ambulance men found him,
as the emergency services had inevitably been
phoned up, as they always were. Surely he was
having a heart attack, didn't they think?

*

Anything can trigger off an attack in people
who suffer from the condition. Lack of sleep,
too much booze, excitement, racing thoughts,
coffee, anger. In Jimmy's case it was usually the
Edinburgh Festival, or rather the aftermath, and
he well remembered the first time it happened,
in the middle of watching television in his
girlfriend's London flat, on the day after his
return from the grey metropolis of the north to
that – the black metropolis of the south.

From nine days of reporting events, where he felt

himself transported from hell to heaven, where his white shirt remained white and not black after an hour's wear, where tap water didn't look like petrol, and – gloriously! – the other water lathered at first wash – he found himself surrounded by five paramedics, a stretcher, a fairly useless blanket, and a face on Ginny so mournful, so worried, so concerned, so in love, that even in his gaga state, his utter confusion, he had to smile, and say like a reflection of Florence Nightingale: "Too kind! Too kind!" The junior doctor examined him. Simple things. The sharp stick on the underside of the foot, the hammer on the knee, the pencil and the eye. All basic reflex stuff. "You'll live," he said, "but you'll have to come back for tests."

2

It took weeks of course, for the tests to be set up. The blood tests, for God knows what. The EEG. The CAT scan. The X-rays. To Jimmy, the answer was obvious. A brain tumour. Only twenty-six, and this was his dismissal.

There would be surgery, naturally.

They would poke about in his head – and he had heard that you had to be fully conscious as they sawed through the skull, cut through all the surrounding protection, the dura mater, the pia mater, until they reached the cerebral cortex, where they would slice out the thing, whatever size it was, a pea, a golf ball, a tennis ball, an orange. He would be left a vegetable, simpering and smiling all day long, while the tumour regrew either in his brain, or somewhere else more sinister and painful, the spine, the bones, the liver, until he died, singing continuously the death rattle of the new age, some ad jingle from his youth – 'Wrigley's Spearmint Gum, Gum,

Gum!' or 'Boom-boom-boom-boom, Esso Blue!'

This much was certain. It was a depressing
business. He must put his affairs in order, that
is, if he had had any affairs.

Ginny told what happened. "We were watching
Coronation Street. Now I know you don't like
Corrie, but I have to put up with your news
programmes and I'm sure you'll get into it one
day, you seem to know all the characters though.

"– no, Jimmy, Amy Turtle's dead, and anyway
she wasn't in Coronation Street, she was in
Crossroads.

"– anyway, like, your eyes all glazed over, and
you collapsed straight down, not slouched
or anything like that, wallop! – and then you
started jittering around, foaming at the mouth,
blood coming out. It was horrible. I thought
you were having a heart attack. I phoned for an
ambulance straight away. They took you to St
Thomas's. You were talking nonsense, but then
that's nothing new."

*

St Thomas's is an old institution, but the hospital
on the South Bank of the Thames opposite the
Houses of Parliament, was newly-built. "At
the cutting edge," noted Jimmy ruefully, as
he bargained with his God for his life, in the
cafeteria.

"I'll do work for charity," he prayed, "I'll raise
thousands of pounds for brain tumour research,
O God, if I don't have one."

3

He had put on his Edinburgh University tie,
since the consultant's name was MacAllister,
and though he didn't expect superior treatment,
looking vaguely educated would perhaps mean
no soft soap or idiot talk.

The specialist was a silver-haired, distinguished-
looking man, with the gold-rimmed, half-moon
spectacles favoured by the professions. He stood
with his back to Jimmy, examining some plates
on a light display unit, which looked like X-rays,
or CAT-scans, or whatever.

"Ever had a head injury?"

"Yes"

"When?"

"Five years ago. On my twenty-second birthday.
I was pushed down some steps by a man in Leith,
who took exception to my dinner jacket, and
perhaps me singing a local ditty, then popular on
the radio for some reason."

"What was the song?"

"I think it went 'Hearts! Hearts! Glorious
Hearts!'"

"Not a clever song to sing in Leith," he said with
an accent much changed but still recognisable
Scottish. "I see you went to Edinburgh, Glasgow
myself."

A mistake thought Jimmy, fiddling with his tie
– now the bastard's going to enjoy telling me my
fate.

"Were you in hospital?"

"Yes. A taxi driver took me to the Royal Infirmary, where they kept me in for observation. I was bleeding from the scalp. I got myself sprung after two days."

"Fractured skull?"

"They said it was. But they had no CAT-scans then. I think they have now."

"I see," he said, smiling.

The neurologist turned around to the light display: "Look at this."

"Yes."

"Brain damage. Very minor brain damage. No more than a bruise If it had been here" – he pointed his stick to a few centimetres down – "you wouldn't be able to talk." He moved his pointer around.

"Luckily, it was there."

The doctor changed his mood.

"You've had an epileptiform attack."

"Grand mal?" said Jimmy.

"Whatever it was it was certainly mal. If it recurs, we might have to put you on pills, or something else. Moderate your alcohol consumption, get plenty of sleep. Don't overdo it."

"You mean, I don't have a tumour?"

4

"Heavens no, whatever made you think that?"
said the consultant: "Now I have other people to
see... "

*

It is a delightful state to be in. It is death in
life, yet it is not death, nor more than life. It
is golden this moment. Shaking, falling. It is
the state of the priests and medicine men and
shamans of long ago. It is, they say, a stigma.
Wine, bathing in wine. Not for me it is no
stigma. It is not nothing. It is fine. Showering
in heaven. Golden wine. Saunating. Wake up.
Groggy. Ambulance men.

The registrar examined him. "Jimmy," he said,
after he had used his pointer on the soles of
the feet, on the eye, on the knee. "We can offer
surgery for this. We can cure you. All it requires
is a small operation on the brain."

Jimmy looked at him with the love of Ginny
several years before. "Too kind!" he said. "Too
kind!"

Above: The One O'Clock Gun Spot-The-
Stereotype Challenge, from Number 13. The
Edina 'literary scene' assembled in Rutherfords
Bar, as imagined by Lucy: 13 stereotypical lovers/
loathers of the OOCG.

Can you identify who is who and which is which
– perhaps you'll even recognise yourself!

Solution on page 283.

Your Poems Are Gay

By Keith Farquhar

"Your poems are gay."

That's what my friend
MacIsaac would say.

But I definitely don't think you're a homo.

You're meek!
So what!

It's not judgement day!
And it's not that you're really gay!

But you try...

And I really do think that your output is weak.

Diamonds Deep Beneath The Mountain Range

By Gav Duvet

Amidst the darkness you are wide awake.

Just like the diamonds deep beneath the
    mountain range.

Just like the brightest spark in the universe.

And, amidst the darkness when I cannot see you,
I feel your arched palm rock slowly on mine and,
as it sails to my face, I feel your breath upon my
cheek.

And, when you are gone and you are dearly
missed, it will be the same and you won't, truly,
have left.

Amidst the darkness you will be wide awake.

Just like the diamonds deep beneath the
    mountain range.

Just like the brightest spark in the universe.

And, amidst the darkness when I cannot see you,
I will feel your arched palm rock slowly on mine
and, as it sails to my face, I will feel your breath
upon my other cheek.

Tattie

By Craig Gibson

Whilst out on my deliveries recently I noted with some amusement that Oddfellows in Forrest Road had once again opened its doors after a long, forgettable stint as an Aussie bar. Oddfellows was, in the late eighties and early nineties, something of an underage drinkers' Mecca. I'm sure many Edina thirtysomethings will fondly remember cutting their drinking teeth in 'Oddies' if they could get past the doormen. And for working class gets like myself, the place was absolutely hoaching with posh totty, the likes of which were rarely encountered in Leith.

Oddly enough (pardon the pun) as I sat sipping a pint over the road in Sandy Bell's, my reminiscences did not concern these delightfully conceited, confident beauties of yesteryear, but rather a sad nae-mates individual nicknamed Tattie who was often to be found on Oddies' balcony on his lonesome, surveying the meat market below with what I'm sure he regarded as a sardonic eye.

He was always the butt of everyone's jokes in the traditional role of the village idiot and provided much in the way of the cruel humour that appeals to the young. The reason for this was that no matter how shite your clothes were, and how unconfident you felt in strange new surroundings, if you stood next to him you always looked and felt like a million dollars. Allow me to describe Tattie in more detail.

*

This was the era of acid house and proper indie

music and the club scene was pretty thriving. Therefore, most of the kids at Oddies dressed appropriately, a mixture of dressing up and dressing down, jeans and t-shirts or something more sophisticated depending on where they were going later. However, these sartorial developments seemed to have passed Tattie by – his mode of dress was firmly stuck in the early eighties, when AIDS was still known as GRID, and he was so ridiculous that on more than one occasion we discussed whether or not he was some kind of avant-garde performance artist doing his thing. But he was not.

Without fail, come Friday and Saturday night Tattie would be resplendent in a black fleck suit of poor quality with the sleeves rolled up, Miami Vice style, a black shirt, a slim leather piano-key motif tie with matching black leather gloves (indoors), white socks and a pair of cheap black oxfords. If this wasn't bad enough he had uninteresting hair and a huge chin with an underbite, which earned him his moniker. All he lacked, if looking like a fucking twat was his goal, was a pencil moustache and a pair of fake Raybans perched on his head. He used to act fairly macho into the bargain, standing on the balcony nodding slowly as if he'd seen it all before.

However, as with the rest of us, his stomping ground was not confined to Oddies and no matter how much stick he received, you just couldn't get rid of the boy. There you'd be at the launch night of a trendy club, perhaps sporting a new top and trainers, feeling pretty louche as you knocked back a can of Red Stripe Crucial Brew and you'd turn around to spot Tattie at the bar, dressed in his usual manner, nursing a half pint of cider. No, you couldn't help but meet him in the most unexpected places and you had no choice but to admire his tenacity.

I had no idea a glottal stop, or lack of one, could
provide so much humour until Tattie unwittingly
helped to prove otherwise. A few of us were
having a swell night of it in one of those cavernous
clubs in Victoria Street. As good Scottish boys,
we were accustomed to addressing Tattie (when
we could be bothered) in the Scottish fashion i.e.
with a glottal stop. Coinciding perfectly with a
round of poppers, we heard from the next booth
a frightful shriek emanating from a middle-class
harpie for whom a glottal stop would have been
anathema.

"You're not coming to my party TaTTie!"

We almost pissed ourselves laughing as we
realised that some words should on no account
be pronounced with an English accent, though
admittedly we were having fun, as usual, at
Tattie's expense. However, his customary
doggedness won through and I was not surprised
when only a few minutes later we heard the same
voice state: "Oh yah, TaTTie's coming!"

*

Although it was conceivable that Tattie only
owned a single set of clothes, this theory was
found to be a fallacy when he did eventually
adopt a change of image one night as the new
decade beckoned. We were slightly taken aback
when we saw the familiar chin above unfamiliar
apparel. This new look comprised a badly cut,
snow-washed denim two-piece, a PLO style scarf
wrapped around his neck and a pair of no-mark
white trainers, a kind of 'Shaky meets Aha' look.
The shite haircut and half pint of cider were all
that remained from his previous incarnation, but
he still looked like a walking abortion. Tongues

firmly in our cheeks, we congratulated him on his new threads.

"Aye," was his reply, lacking any semblance of irony. "If this doesnae work, then it's back tae the poser claes."

I've always pondered what Tattie meant by 'work'. I assume he was referring to acquiring a bird, mates, respect etc, but maybe I'm wrong. Perhaps he had loftier goals, though I suspect that he would have settled for the above. Anyway, I have no idea if the image change worked for I had begun to outgrow Oddies by this time and my interest in clubbing had waned, so I rarely saw him again.

Mind you, he never reverted to the 'poser claes' as far as I am aware, so who can tell?

An excerpt from: How Ages Die

By R A Jamieson

From the top flat window in the summer, looking
out over the treetops, you might just walk across
them to the far side of the park – if only you
could make it to the first tree safely, the one
where the crows have nested.

But she's in one corner, him in another, back to
back. She's surfing to find if her favourite big
guy scored at the weekend in Moscow, the one
she used to watch with Dad at Easter Road.

He's watching a thing on that woman, the
yachtswoman who's a MacArthur, same as his
mother's side. He admires her independence,
wonders how anyone could be alone so totally,
then checks the paper for the pick of the day.

In the kitchen the dryer is merging their fabrics,
leg twisting into sleeve, crotch into armpit, warp
to woof. And she forgot to take out that blouse,
the green one that runs.

*

She flings the window open, to the call rising
upwards, of some young gun on the pitch and
putt, above the squeals from the playpark:

Get tae fuck, ya fuck ya, will yae?

The mouths on them, you'd never believe they
were the bairns of Ma an Pa.

The Lost Superhero

By Kirsti Wishart

Cathy had loved him since she was very small,
before she even knew his name, before she
discovered there were people called cartoonists
who worked in offices to produce these wonderful
things called comics that appeared magically on
newsagent shelves every Thursday morning.

It started when she was four years old and found
a copy of Amazing Tales that had sneaked into a
box of Twinkles and Buntys kept at the nursery.
Her first exposure to the stable of Colt Comics,
she'd pleaded with her mum to ask the nursery
assistant to let her take it home. She'd kept it until
the pages turned soft and had to be held together
by sellotape and although it was a while before she
could read all the words in the speech bubbles,
the pictures were excitement enough. She thrilled
to the adventures of Dr Dual, The Whisperer and
Mekanoids! but the story that held her attention,
the one she kept folded and safe in the back of one
of her favourite books after the rest of the comic
had disintegrated, was his – The Lost Superhero.

Back then she'd loved it for being set in the city
she knew, its locations rendered in exquisite
detail – the City Museum, the Railway Station,
the Ornamental Baths. As she grew older she
began to appreciate the emotional force of the
story; a man who had lived during the glory years
of the city, who, in the City Labs, had developed
superhuman abilities while forging ahead with
scientific advancement. With these powers he had
sought to protect the people of the city, ridding
the streets of crime and violence. With time,
however, his strength had faded and he was left to
wander the streets, visiting the sites of his greatest

victories against his arch-villains – The Man With No Face, Terminal Rage and The Commander, all either dead or in nursing homes for the criminally insane.

The potentially bleak subject matter was leavened by the small discoveries made as he walked the city at night, chatting to other lost souls in the bus station, entering an unlocked gate to find private gardens turned magical by moonlight, discovering the best cup of coffee ever at an all-night Turkish café. These things he shored up against the depression felt as he witnessed what he regarded as the city's decline, a decline matching his own physical deterioration; the rubbish on the streets, the graffiti, the muggings.

But as Cathy began to develop her own cartooning talent, she saw to the heart of the comic, read it as a love song to urban life, a lyrical celebration of its strange juxtapositions and pockets of neglected beauty. Although she suspected his name a pseudonym, an anagram perhaps, she grew to love Stanley D. Wikudd, the cartoonist who wrote and drew the strip, seeking out his work and what little biographical information there was. Although she enjoyed her years at the city's Art College, she felt she'd learnt all she needed from studying the panels of The Lost Superhero and that her near complete collection of Amazing Tales was a greater resource than the college library.

Through talking to other fans met in second-hand comic shops she learnt more about Stanley, how he'd learnt to draw by copying bubblegum stickers while sitting under the counter of his Dad's tobacconist shop. He'd chosen to work for Colt Comics, despite offers from the mighty Webb Publications, the city's most powerful publisher, because they afforded him a greater degree of freedom, allowing him to produce work in his own eccentric way. His work would never be edited, the level of detail would never be compromised to save on printing costs and the only contact he would have with the Colt Comic offices was when hand-delivering the final storyboard a minute before the weekly deadline.

Few people could give an eye-witness account of Stanley's appearance but for some reason Cathy felt sure he'd depicted himself wandering in the background of the Lost Superhero. Sometimes in the Central Library, the Art Gallery or on one of her own night-walks, she would see a man who looked faintly familiar, wearing an old-fashioned rain-coat and flat-cap and wonder if it was him, the great Stanley Wikudd ignored and anonymous and happy that way, collecting information for his latest story.

The announcement of the take-over of Colt Comics by Webb Publications shocked ardent comic fans. Webb's was responsible for such bland hits as Housewife's Choice and Coffee Time and while press releases stated Colt Comics would retain their individuality few believed the claim. The announcement took place on Cathy's Graduation Day, overshadowing the celebrations as clusters of newly qualified cartoonists nervously discussed their future at the Ball. They knew Colt's maverick approach that had attracted experimental talents would be lost, the edgy creativity that saw Colt Comics lead the way in innovation, pushing the boundaries of censorship, made safe and audience-friendly.

Worse was to come with a letter published on page three of the City Gazette a week later. Signed 'Stanley D. Wikudd' it protested in the strongest possible terms to the take-over, warning it would have dire consequences for the development of the city's cartooning talent. But the paragraph that made the letter news was the one in which Stanley committed himself to refusing publication of any of his strips by Webb. As Webb Publications now held a virtual monopoly of the city's publishers this effectively meant the Lost Superhero would truly live up to his name.

There were some who argued in the booths of The Red Rocket Bar, the main drinking den of the city's cartoonists, that this was a publicity stunt. Where was the proof this letter had actually been written by Wikudd? But when the new, revamped edition of Amazing Tales appeared, retitled Amaze! in a larger format on glossier paper, the only talking point was the absence of The Lost Superhero. Stanley had held true to his promise.

A week later Cathy sat in the snug of The Red Rocket on a quiet afternoon, holding a letter from Webb Publications offering her a job as a colourist on Mekanoids! one of the few Colt titles to be retained. She sipped her pint and tried to hold back her tears. She knew this was a fantastic opportunity, but the sadness at the loss of one of her great cartooning heroes couldn't be eased. What made it worse was certainty that by accepting the job she would be betraying her idol. She tried to cheer herself up by studying the wall opposite. Here all the cartoonists who had passed through the Rocket's doors had left their mark, adding sketches of their characters or favourites scenes from comics past and present until the entire wall was covered, one huge cartoon palimpsest.

Staring at it, her vision blurred by emotion and alcohol Cathy blinked and then blinked again. For a moment the drawings of Astro And Frou, Spaceships Of Love, Krazy Kat and hundreds of other well-loved and long forgotten characters had become something else, something more.

Another, larger picture emerging from the layering of images, an order imposed on the seemingly random. Then it was gone until she squinted and saw it for definite; the ghost of an image but a ghost nonetheless. A man in a raincoat, the collar turned up, hair slicked back, peering over the top of a comic. The Lost Superhero himself wearing a wicked grin, staring at her. She blinked and he vanished.

"Did you see?" she murmured, more to herself than anyone else, not expecting an answer. So when a man's voice said, "Finally! You've found him, about bloody time!" she turned, shocked.

She'd been dimly aware of a man sitting in the corner of the room when she'd entered, his head bowed, completing a crossword. Now he was sitting on the seat next to her, watching her with a strange intensity. He was one of the older crowd of Rocket regulars but whereas they were generally red-faced eccentrics, his face had a studied blandness to it. It was as if he'd deliberately decided to make it as unremarkable, as unmemorable as possible. But his eyes told a different story; bright and quick, practiced in absorbing as much information as possible in the shortest available time. And as soon as she saw them she knew who he was.

"Stanley?" she whispered, the breath knocked out of her by excitement. "Hmm," he replied, giving the briefest of nods, looking away as if embarrassed and when his gaze left her it was like a light switched off. "But – I mean – are you really? Because you're the reason I'm – "

"Yes, yes," he muttered, his discomfort making clear the reasons behind his decision to steer clear of office life. "I don't have time for all that. And you've seen enough already, the picture on the wall.

Remember what I said in my letter to the paper.
I won't be published by any major publisher again,"
and his eyes flicked up to her, halting any attempt
at interruption, "but I didn't say anything about
smaller publications, free-sheets, underground
press, whatever you want to call it. I've been
watching you closely Cathy Gunn – "

"– but how did you know – ?"

He waved his hand, brushing the query aside, "and
I know what you're capable of. You get yourself
a proper job, be a wage slave. But there's other
work you know you should be doing, other work
you know you have to do if you're to keep the
imagination of this city alive. I'll be watching and
when you're ready, he'll be back to walk the streets
again," he said, tipping his head in the direction of
the wall.

"But – " and Cathy was stopped by Stanley
standing up abruptly, picking up the raincoat by
his side, putting on a bunnet that must have been
old in the 1930s, making clear he had said all he
was going to say.

"Just stop dithering, woman, and get on with it.
I'll be in touch but when... well, that's down to
you," and with that he was gone, the front door of
the Rocket left swinging in his wake.

She thought about getting up, running after him,
asking him all the questions she'd been saving
since she was four or even just what the 'D' stood
for. Instead she sat, thinking for a minute or two
before hoisting her bag on to her lap and pulling
out her sketchbook and pen. She started to work,
drawing up a masthead, a layout, writing out a list
of names. And she didn't have to look up to know
the Lost Superhero was there, watching, found at
last, readying himself to walk again.

Growing Up & Moving On

By Gerry Hillman

The 2001 census indicated that the population
of Edinburgh was 453,430; since then I can
only assume that the necessary 46,570 have
been born/moved here to make us half-million-
merchants. The reason for making this glib
sounding assumption is simple: Edinburgh has
recently been behaving suspiciously like a real,
gen-up European city, and I can't help but feel
that this is a simple matter of mathematics –
once you cross a certain boundary of population,
certain behaviours manifest themselves in that
population.

1) The street dope dealer. When I first went
to London on my own (i.e. not with my folks),
about 12 years ago, the first thing I did to assert
my masculine adulthood (as I saw it) was to
purchase some grass from a street dealer. He
was walking down Camden High Street or some
similarly hippified part of North London (the
girl I was there with knew enough to know that
Camden was the place to head for wannabe heads
like us) asking the legendary, if ungrammatical
question "good weed, Man?" Of course I said
"Yes, please". Of course the weed was probably
mediocre. Of course the deal was probably
appalling. Of course I felt amazing just for having
scored at all, although I have no recollection
how stoned or not I got. So... fast forward to
a month ago, I'm walking down Albert Street
and those same beautiful words come echoing
through the mists of time: "good weed, Man?"
This time, alas, I felt I had to just say "No". Still,
I felt amazing just knowing that Edinburgh was
coming of age enough to have street dope dealer
dudes like in super-cool Camden Town.

2) The street other-stuff seller. Not sure what to say, here, apart from, it was like being on holiday on the continent. Me and The Editor were bevvying in Maggie Middleton's when I accompanied him outside when he went for a fag so as not to break the conversational flow. We're standing there talking whatever shite when a polite older lady came and butted in: "would you like to buy a ring?" – the puzzlement we felt was obviously manifest on our faces, as she removed from a patterned hankie a selection of non-precious-metal rings: "For your girlfriend – or wife?"... no we didn't spend our limited bevvy cash on delightful gifts for our ladyfolk, but as we settled back into our seats in the boozer we were feeling more cosmopolitan than we had done for some time – living in a European capital city wasn't such an unrealistic dream after all... we were already getting there...

3) The shopfront cab firm. This time to Coronation Street, where they've had a shopfront cab firm for ages. You know the sketch: you walk in, tell them where you're off to, decide a price, wait for a dodgy two grand Ford Sierra to appear to take you home or wherever. While in London this strange business is called a Minicab (to distinguish it I suppose from the optimistically named 'Hackney Carriage'), here I can only describe it as blow against the pettiness and parochialism for which Edinburgh was once known – although, as I demonstrate, we move further beyond this daily. Man, I would need to be truly desperate for a cab to bother with such an establishment, but its presence as I walk past, complete with drivers waiting outside, smoking fags, bantering, waiting for a fare, etc, gives me the feeling that I'm in a feature-length made-for-TV film about living in the Big City. I like that feeling very much.

4) Crap stuff. Obviously, crap stuff is not new to Edinburgh, but there are new types of crap stuff which are marking us out as joining the big-league of citidom. Tiny flats costing half-a-million-quid; Five pound pints of lager; Football teams owned by insane Russian Oligarchs; Nightclubs getting a guest DJ so selling advance tickets for £20... you know the style. The great thing about these types of crap stuff is that the seasoned pro can feel wonderfully smug: "go in there for a £5 pint? Nah – there's a cool place just round the corner where it's half the price and the beer's better..." or "you paid how much for your place? you're insane, we rent just across the road from that and it's a tenth of the price!" If the crap stuff wasn't crap, there'd be no benefit to being a local, feeling like the kind of cool guy who could show a tourist the REAL Edinburgh.

5) Self referential articles in free broadsheets. One of the real signs of Edinburgh's coming of age is the growth in self-referential articles in free quarterly broadsheets: we have recently come to believe that Edinburgh is like London or somewhere – one can namedrop streets in Leith like they're Park Lane, mention obscure boozers as if they're the Coach and Horses or Harry's Bar. It takes a city of a certain size to assume that level of self-aggrandisement and then to celebrate it openly... so, here's to ever-growing, ever-growing-up Edinburgh and long may it continue to surprise us with the rich tapestry of weirdness which inspires us. I look forward to seeing what genius new stuff comes with the next transition: when we hit 1,000,000 and join Lima, Birmingham, Lagos etc in the real big league!

Sandy Meets The One O'Clock Gun

By Sandy Christie

The Commoners' Guide To The New Town Pleasure Gardens

By Craig Gibson

A few issues ago I contributed a flight of fancy entitled The New Town Vampire to the pages of the Gun. A whimsical affair but, if you will permit me to blow my own trumpet for a second, I reckon it painted a far more realistic portrayal of New Town values than Sandy McSmith's weedy efforts in the Scotsman.

Anyway, I already had the story written in my head, more or less, but I supposed it might be a good idea to conduct some research. The private gardens of the New Town (where the tale was largely set) were a bit of a mystery to me. I didn't know any key holders and the thought of getting caught or injured whilst trying to climb over the railings was anathema. I'm in my late thirties for fuck's sake and the shame would have been the death of me.

Fortunately, a close colleague and Gun stalwart provided me with a cunning method of entry. He furnished me with a brass bottle/can opener and assured me that the slim little beauty could pop the locks of the majority of the gates protecting the gardens if one possessed the requisite skill. I swiftly proceeded to learn the craft and am now a smug, satisfied, self-styled locksmith, able to come and go as I please, for once my research was complete I had fallen in love with the gardens and was determined to use them with impunity.

I will describe the method and other details below, but I want to make it clear at this point that I am not advocating a mass invasion of the gardens by the great unwashed. I really don't want these havens to be accessible to the public, for I do not believe their fragile beauty would survive and I thoroughly detest crowds. The yearly fee for the privilege of renting a key is astronomical, I am told, which is why the gardens are generally enjoyed only by the fortunate few. The status quo is fine by me, nonetheless, for I am no Marxist revolutionary and enjoy having a few special spots around town where I can smoke, drink and think in isolated splendour. But if you're keen, and discretion is your watchword, here she blows:

The Gardens:
The pleasure gardens of the New Town are superb places to relax, the best in town, and a joy to explore. Although they are all undoubtedly beautiful, the real jewel has to be the garden between Howe Street and Dundas Street, in which you can meditate by the very pond where RLS played as a boy (the most sacred site in literary Edina). Consult an A-Z if you are unsure of their exact locations, for there are gardens scattered all over the New Town. Nevertheless, from Moray Place to Drummond Place, one must gain entry first.

Reconnaissance:
So, first of all, choose a gate and give her a shake. If she doesn't shake, rattle and roll then it's no go, so try another one. If she does, you're in with a chance. Now, all you need is a tool, some patience and a little talent. If you are attempting to breach the gardens during rush hour then a brass neck would probably help too. Keep a mental map of which gates go and which do not – this should save you a lot of messing around in the future. Once you have opened a particular gate, there is no reason to suspect you will be unable to do so again and again.

Equipment:
To pop the locks with style you have to be tooled
up in an appropriate manner. I originally
used the tool described above, but I have also
fashioned implements from a credit card and a
customised pair of tweezers. All of these tools
are 100% legal and you are breaking no law
whatsoever by possessing them. Basically any
slim, semi-flexible, blunt device will suffice – the
mind boggles, so have fun experimenting. I have
found that some tools succeed where others fail,
as all locks are unique, so it is probably advisable
to carry a selection at all times.

The Method:
It is vital to be able to get into the back of the
lock, which is why an unshakeable gate is a
non-starter. The method is in fact fairly simple,
although it does require a bit of practice. Pull
the gate towards you as tight as you can with
one hand while slipping your other hand holding
a chosen implement through the bars. There
should be just enough space to enable you
to wiggle the implement into the back of the
lock. Keep wiggling and within a few seconds
or minutes, depending on your ability, the gate
shall open as if by magic. Normally, you have to
rely on your sense of touch alone, in an almost
Zen fashion, although some of the gates at the
East End are short enough for you to look over
and actually see what you are doing. These
gates are ideal for beginners. Of course, the
act of popping the lock does look suspicious
(and frankly, illegal) but this is only a problem
when you are on the outside. The real beauty
of the method is that when you are exiting the
gardens you can see the lock completely and
it looks as though you are legitimately using
a key to any curtain-twitchers. Please note
that some of the gardens may be hip to this,
however. Drummond Place is particularly well

guarded – all of its gates are protected by a wire mesh that capably prevents devious hands from performing. If you are determined to explore this one, I'm afraid it's an over-the-railings job, though I'm pretty sure they lack spikes.

Security:
I have never encountered anyone resembling an authority figure during my illicit rambles. As far as I am aware there is no such thing as a park patrol, though at first I was a little paranoid that someone would demand to see my key. This plebian paranoia was completely unfounded as, in typical New Town fashion, other users usually keep to themselves and ask no questions. I have only spoken with one genuine key holder sporting what looked like cricket whites, who remarked it was "marvellous living in Abercrombie Place, no?", but I have no way of knowing if he was testing my partner and me, or if he was just being friendly on a balmy summer evening. As I have previously noted, the gardens are normally chronically empty in any case, the most frequent daily visitors being au-pairs, yummy mummies and dog walkers. As long as you are not creating a disturbance you will be left completely unmolested, which brings me to my last topic.

Responsibility:
Once inside the gardens it is wise to behave as if you own them. These beautiful lush, green acres are yours to leisurely explore and only idiots would despoil their own sanctuary (or shit in their own nest, to be frank). Therefore, to quote Stephen Sondheim, play it cool. If you intend to partake of some alcoholic refreshment, go for a few fancy continental beers or a nice bottle of wine with glasses. Avoid cheap cider, super strength lager, Buckfast or any other sort of tramp juice. Mobs of rowdy drunks will increase

New Town vigilance, I fear, and this could lead to some kind of crackdown on clandestine activities. If you must drink and act like a jakey then I suggest your interests would be better served up in West Princes Street Gardens or, let's face it, the Tron. Smoke discreetly and remove all litter including fag butts and roaches. Attract as little attention as possible and, when promenading, I recommend clasping your hands behind your back in the manner of the Duke of Rothesay (this will give you an air of respectability). I implore anyone who chooses to employ my method to treat the gardens with utmost reverence, so resourceful commoners with dexterous fingers may continue to infiltrate Edina's very own slice of Eden for many years to come.

The Slaughterer Of St Stephen Street

By Gavin Inglis

Some say the Slaughterer of St Stephen Street
was simply a story; a shameless scam synthesized
by some scoundrel. Yet stoic souls swear to its
sincerity.

In 1866 a shopkeeper was suspicious of a solitary
silhouette stumbling along St Stephen Street
at sunset. He spoke to the stranger sharply.
Startled, the shape seized him and strangled him
with savage strength. He was soon sprawled on
the shop's steps.

This was the second in a series of slayings; skulls
were smashed, servants stabbed and spinsters
succumbed to a sinister spectre who stalked the
sophisticated sections of Stockbridge. He seemed
a supernatural specimen; a Satanic scavenger,
shambling and sneaking to strike, smashing and
slicing with senseless severity. Some said he was
stout; some, shallow and shifty. These scurrilous
sayings aside, the strip stayed spattered scarlet
with sanguinous spray.

Speculation that the slaughterer studied as a
surgeon was significant when a scalpel was
spotted, stuck into the shoulder of some sad
stiff on the second Sunday of September.
Superstitious scum said somebody with the
second sight had seen scissors slashing a stomach,
snaring and snipping with serious skill. The
Sabbath was squandered in sordid speculation.

The slaughterer was sensationally shown to be
Sir Sidney Sackson, seized as he sawed at the

234

spine of a suicide's skeleton in Surgeons' Hall. The sceptics subdued when shown that Sir Sidney sleepwalked, silently struggling with his subconscious, suffering with some suppressed sorrow, shivering, sweating and shuddering.

Solicitors searched for a solution to the strange scandal of the somnambulistic slaughterer. Speaking with sepulchral solemnity, they suggested a scheme of scrutiny in a secure shelter.

Sadly, he was sent to the solitary section of a sanitarium.

Moira Knox

By Robin Cairns

Moira Knox
Preserve us from the pox
Save us from the people who tie ballast to their
    cocks
Ban the so-called comics who just peddle filth
    and crudity
And Moira, Moira! What about the nakedness,
    the nudity
The ruddy, scuddy cheeks of it
Dangly bits and droopy tits
Three full porny weeks of it
From Bruntsfield to Comelybank it's brazen flesh
    exposure
From Dumbiedykes to Colonies the Fringe is due
    for... Councillor Knox... closure!
Lock them up. Make them get a job
Bare feet. Hairy meat. Buttock, bollock, knob
I wouldn't mind so much if it was ever scuddy
    girls
But it's skinny English Nigels and Jeremys and
    Cyrils
And rough old lezzie rug-munchers doing the
    trapeze
Their boobs are up beyond their ears and then
    below their knees
Moira, Moira! Deliver us from Sodom
Kinky degenerates who want you to applaud 'em
For "foregrounding their transgressive sexuality
    in a challenging adaptation of... Moby Dick!"
Take the buggers out the back and beat them
    with a stick
"Ronaldo the Regurgitator in his show You Make
    Me Sick
Involves bad smells and strobe lights
Bring your own towel!"
Moira! Referee! Simon fuckin Cowell!

If this is entertainment then there ought to be a
    law
Fun is fun but nonsense is poets in the raw
Arse crack, spotty back, funny pubic hair
Moira Knox you stand alone between us and
    despair
It's an Edinbomination to disgrace the Scottish
    nation for a fruitcake to swing a tin of
    shortbread from his member
So Dear Moira, gentle Tory, kick up scandal and
    furore
Cos I'll not be back my holidays til sometime in
    September.

North/South

Days Of 2007

By James Wood

This distance between us:
The echo and delay
Of words and pictures
Lost in whispers.
Somewhere through a mirror
Sun slants off sea
And grey columns cloud over
These ultra-blue waters.
From Forth to Aegean
The magic is holding
Each brush and pen
Tells a promise unspoken:
That some young talent
Will craft a giant heart
To swallow our sorrows
And sketch a fresh start.

No Exit

By Andrew J Wilson

I might have only met Shane Morris once, but that was enough.

"You know how some songs just keep going round and round in your head?" he said. "Well, life does that too sometimes."

The musician downed his JD and Coke, signalling for another like a drowning man waving for a life-belt. I poured his drink and slid it across the bar.

"How many have I had, sweetheart?" he asked.

"Enough," I replied. "And I'm not your sweetheart."

Shane grinned crookedly, only the right side of his mouth rising to the challenge. "You said that the last time, Amy."

"Shane, we've never met before," I pointed out, wondering how he knew my name.

He sank his refill and waved at me again just as I was about to call last orders.

"Yes we have – many times."

Shane was a wannabe rock star who thought he was the next big thing. The punters at the club seemed to agree, but I wasn't convinced the world needed another baby-faced bad boy.

"Look," I told him, "it's late, you're drunk and I've got to clear up. I could do without an argument with someone I don't even know. Go home."

"You think I'm a tosser, don't you?" I walked away, heading for the pepper spray I kept hidden under the other end of the bar. "Well, you're right."

I turned round again.

"I'm going to record one of the biggest-selling albums of the decade, but I'm also going to get hooked on smack. I'm going to see my pregnant girlfriend die from an overdose. Then I'm going to top myself a year later..."

"All right," I said slowly, taking the bait when I should have known better, "and you know this because..."

"Because what they say about your whole life flashing before your eyes when you're dying is really true."

"But you're not dying, are you?"

"I wasn't, not the first time I talked to you – but we've done this a hundred times..." Shane looked sick. "What they don't tell you is that it just keeps happening – it's your whole life, so when you get to the end of the flashback, it happens all over again... but faster every time."

I watched him closely, looking for a sign that he was winding me up.

"Help me," he pleaded, "or I'll keep reliving my life forever."

But I couldn't, of course, so he simply finished his drink, and walked out of the club and out of my life.

As you know, he was telling the truth – it all

came true. But our single encounter still haunts me because, if he was right about everything else, maybe he was right about the flashbacks. Shane will always be trapped in a vicious circle, living his life over and over, faster and faster, never reaching the finish line. Even though it's a kind of immortality, I don't envy him.

I just pray we don't meet again when my time comes.

Above: Roll up! Roll up! Lucy McKenzie's sinister ringmaster welcomes readers to Number 16.

Uncle

By Andrew Smith

"Good evening Nephew."

"Good evening Uncle."

He is not my uncle and I am not his nephew, but we'll come to that part later.

Uncle has gold-rimmed spectacles which, when not perched deftly on the bridge of his nose, hang from a gold chain round his neck. Uncle has white, highly reflective teeth, which shine under the ultra-violet strip lights of certain bars in the city, or in the pale silver light of the moon. Today Uncle has awoken in an exuberant mood, which I do not share. He takes a deep, nostril-flaring inhalation, and treads carefully to the window, where he draws back the heavy curtain by the merest amount, and peers out. When he turns to me again, there is a strange radiance in his smile.

"So Nephew, do I find you in good health and spirits, rested and prepared for the rigours ahead?"

I do not reply and avoid his eyes, preferring to stare wistfully at the milk, which I am pouring dutifully into first his, and then my, tea. The passing moments linger coldly, unpleasantly. Uncle's voice, when he speaks again, has dropped very slightly in volume, and now has an angular, faintly brittle edge to it.

"Come, come, now, my lad. No sulks I hope. No second thoughts. No..." he pauses and, leaning over the table, pokes me with a bony forefinger,

" ...no losing the faith. Eh?" He laughs quickly and stares at me a moment longer as he plucks sugar from the bowl, dropping one, two, three cubes into the teacup, all the time holding me in the persistence of his gaze. When he speaks again it is cheerily.

"I rather thought that we might go further afield today. You know, pastures new. Virgin territory." He laughs at this last part, repeating it for added effect, and his thin frame shakes with mirth. "Virgin territory. Eh? Virgin! Ha ha ha!" Uncle's eyes are shining, and the blood vessels show vividly against the white of his eyeballs, as they do when his excitement has been raised.

"Uncle... " my own voice surprises me with its smallness, " ...I don't want to... do it any more."

A silence to turn the tea cold, the candle dim.

"You have no choice boy. You have no choice. You will do it. You must do it." His words get bigger yet his voice does not get louder. "There are no options, boy."

I cannot speak. There is bleakness in his words, bleakness in this room. I would cry, but tears are not part of this life now, though I remember how they felt, when my senses knew colour and taste, and form and light. And love. And... life.

"Now... " Uncle's face a dreadful, leering mask. "Rouse our friends from the cellar." He steps to the kitchen door, undoes one lock, another, and pulls it open, quivering as the dark and black night floods in, filling every corner of the room with its ghastly blackness. About me I feel the presence of other bodies, the odour of soil and wood as they crawl past me into the night.

244

And on the sharp points of Uncle's teeth the full moon glows brilliantly. He is not my uncle, and I am not his nephew, but he is my blood relation, and blood is thicker than water, though neither now flows in my withered, lifeless, punctured veins.

The Control

By Ross Wilson

The game was about to start and Dad was about
to reach for the control when Son walked in,
picked it up, and flicked the channel.

What ye dayin? Dad says.

– Wa't? Son goes, turning to face him, waving
the control at the telly.

– The game's aboot tae start, he says.

Dad frowns.

– Mibbe Ah wis watchin somethin.

– Ye wirnae though.

– Hoo dae you ken?

– Well, what wir ye watchin?

– That's no the point! Dad says, standing up and
crossing the room. He snatches the control out
of Son's hand and walks back to his arse-dent in
the couch.

Son tuts as Dad aims the control at the telly.

– The game's aboot tae start, Son mumbles.

So was the Tellytubbies.

Dad frowns at the fat furry 'tubbies as his finger
feathers the buttons on the control, his hand
slowly forming a fist around it, locking the plastic
into his grip.

246

Son frowns, his bottom lip curls.

Dad looks at his watch: the game was about to start.

And the Tellytubbies had a ball and they were singing again!

again!

again!

Upcountry

By Angus Calder

The night of the spider. The morning of the
woman.

I was woken that morning by the noise of a
small vacuum cleaner, cut across by a loud
farewell to his wife from my host Robert.
Though it was only 7am, he was crossing the
road to his work at the college and Miriam was
deep into housework. I knew she had help from
the little local town – and, sure enough, a thin,
tiny, startled woman nearly bumped into me
on the stair as I carried my light case down.
I said good morning, she muttered something,
head down, morosely, and continued up the
stairs, presumably to clean the bedroom and
bathroom which I'd used. But downstairs, order
and cleanliness were already complete. I did
not tell Miriam about the spider, thinking that
she might infer a slur on her cleanliness. And
perhaps her helper would take it for granted,
never mention it.

This had been a minimal safari 'upcountry'.
During my month in this central African nation
– noted for the unflagging viciousness and
hypocrisy of its dictator and its perseverance,
unique on the continent, in open trade and
diplomacy with apartheid South Africa – the
University Department of English, which had
accorded me a visiting lectureship, thought it
might amuse me to give an outpost of academia
some taste of my presumed brilliance. The lucky
institution was basically an agricultural college,
but there was a very limited enrichment of its
syllabus with 'liberal arts', and primary school
teachers were trained there.

I was supplied with an ageing but robust Peugeot 'station wagon' and its chauffeur, John. Though his uniform – cap and black suit, even a tie – was clean and neat, there was something enjoyably piratical about John. I did not trust him. Certain hints from a colleague had persuaded me that he combined driving duties with snooping and spying for the regime. But his gusty conversation relieved the longish drive north under grey skies, and his countenance was dramatised by the fact that, unlike most Africans of his age – about 35 – his teeth were truly terrible: half his front ones gone. One imagined a tavern brawl, probably with a jealous husband – and also some patient and terrible revenge on whoever had hit him.

John dropped me at the Cartwrights' quite commodious bungalow, so close to the College campus, and sped on himself to the little town. From our brief acquaintance, I was absolutely certain that he would use his relative affluence as a university employee to buy himself the bonniest local prostitute and heroic quantities of the (good) local lager. He had told me that the (very good) local gin gave him headaches. So he stuck to lager...

Robert snatched my suitcase, rather nervily, apologised for Miriam's absence ("shopping in town"), took me up to the bedroom I would use, then rushed me over to the college, with just enough time to have sandwiches and coffee before my lecture. Though, or because, packed out with solemn students ordered, no doubt, to be there, the lecture was unsuccessful. Surmising correctly that an upcountry college in this very poor country would be very short of books, I had got a secretary to cyclostyle two foolscap pages of verse by the most distinguished, but also the most obscure, poet in English from West Africa. There were copies

249

enough for one between three students. What was teachable in this country at the University produced blank looks, not very discreet yawns, and no questions afterwards except from Robert. Did I think, he asked, not quite helpfully, that poets of West Africa were closer to readers here than British and American poets? I waffled in response.

So I felt rather low over another cup of coffee with Robert and a couple of colleagues in the utterly graceless common room – walls painted a dull pale blue – where elderly copies of Time and Reader's Digest were the only periodicals on offer. When Robert took me back to his house it seemed by contrast eminently well appointed. Miriam was now there to greet me, and we chatted awhile before I went upstairs to wash.

Their story quickly unfolded for me. Before getting his lectureship here, Robert had taught – geography, as I remember – in a mission school, Anglican, but 'clap-happy' Evangelical, in an adjacent republic. Miriam had been a star pupil – already twenty or so when they met, so entirely marriageable when she completed her schooling. She had been training part-time here as a teacher, but showed for this no enthusiasm. Later, I would believe that I understood why...

Robert was a thoroughly decent fellow, but earnestness rather than humour predominated. He had a pleasant, genteel Yorkshire accent. His spectacles, oddly, were frameless, like pince-nez. With his scant fair hair and thin, prim lips, these helped him seem to embody a Methodistical Northern dourness. His great love was his clarinet, which he had few chances to play in company here. Though he was of an age with me – mid thirties – I fear he was somewhat overawed by my doctorate and my published

250

books. Unwisely, he chose to regale us with a minute account of his college's objectives and curriculum, largely in education-speak, that jargon of departments and colleges of Education, much of which I couldn't follow – so dinner was rather painful, though the food was good straightforward stuff, imported steak with fine home-grown potatoes.

Miriam, maybe thirty, dressed in a white blouse and navy-blue skirt which could have constituted school uniform, said little, but it was always to the point. One gathered that living so close to the college and its halls of residence, she had seized the chance to 'mother' lonely and confused students, rather like Matron in a British boarding school. Normally she was solemn, giving close attention to Robert's words, but her face blazed with life when she talked about her young men. "Titus told me that Geography will be the death of him, so you may be his assassin, Robert... That Jacob, he cares for just two things – football and jam."

The word 'comely' seems to me to suit her. 'Pretty' would be wildly inappropriate. She had short hair au naturel – none of the straightening and perming which hotel whores and the wives of rich Africans went in for. Her features were large – lustrous eyes, strong cheekbones, a very full mouth. She was, I should add, as black as they came in these parts.

She was also, I concluded, brighter than Robert. She picked up his education-speak and found ways of explaining it to me without putting him down.

I had thought to bring a bottle of wine with me – South African, perforce, I am sorry to say – and the Wainwrights had thought in parallel.

251

Since she had just one glass and he only three,
I did rather well for myself and went upstairs
about eleven pleasantly tipsy.

My room was austere but comfortable enough,
with a useful washhand-basin which would spare
me from blundering about in search of the loo.
However, in the centre of the floor there squatted
a monster.

This was the largest spider I had ever seen
– about the size, diametrically speaking, of a
teaplate. It was a rather evil reddish colour.

I thought, it's either him or me.

In a corner I spotted a sizeable carton, full to
the brim with papers, no doubt composed in
education-speak. I seized this and dropped it
from about four feet on the spider. Removing
it, I saw that the beast was utterly squashed,
and with great relief peed, undressed down to
my underwear, went to bed and at once fell
asleep.

When I woke about seven am, my first glance
was towards the centre of the floor. The vista
was discomforting. Only the spider's legs
remained – rather henge-like, ancient in aspect,
a bony monument. All its flesh must have been
consumed by other creatures inhabiting the
room. I had thought myself safe – but what
nastiness and perils might I have evaded by
sheer good fortune? I would inspect my cast-
aside clothes very carefully...

Meanwhile, I lay in for a while, depressed. The
boring weather. My boring lecture. Robert's
near-intolerable conversation. I thought how
glad I would be to get back to base. John was
turning up with the car about eleven. I had

thought that this lateish departure would give me time for further exploration of the campus, but now I couldn't give a damn.

Miriam, the superb housewife, had polished the furniture with something strongly scented, which made me think, correctly I suppose, of pyrethrum. The bottles and crumbs of last night had been purged completely. And Miriam knew what a British man expected at this time of day. I got fresh pawpaw, cornflakes, bacon and sausage (imported) and two eggs (local), followed by toast with margarine and jam. I was offered tea, but opted for instant coffee.

She had changed to a grey blouse and denim skirt, over which she unaffectedly wore an apron. She moved in and out of her kitchen, washing up stage by stage as I gratefully consumed her feast. All that was missing was reading matter. The one English language newspaper permitted in that country had not yet arrived, and in any case it would be so censored as to be virtually worthless. (Around this time – it was 1978 – Nyerere's Tanzanian troops swept into Kampala and deposed the tyrant Amin. This was not reported by the newspaper in question, which had front-page headlines about a cabinet change in Japan. Citizens must not get hold of the idea that tyrants might be overthrown... But those who cared got the news from the BBC World Service.)

With rather more than two hours to kill, I was happy that Miriam should show me the garden. The Cartwrights cultivated more vegetables than flowers, but peas and potatoes are not unattractive. Sun had at last broken through cloud. At a little table with two chairs, we sat and talked as I enjoyed glimpses of passing bright birds.

253

"Do you have children?"

"Yes. Two." I pulled out my wallet and produced a photo.

"Lovely", she said, "Such lovely fair hair." I was surprised by the hint of a sob in her voice.

"What are their names?"

"Adrian and Maria."

"Lovely", again.

Then it all came out. Here she was, 'at her age', with no children. Her family was fertile. She had eight siblings, all from one mother (whose own mother had been an early Christian convert.) Her father, who had migrated annually to the Rand goldmines for work, and ultimately had not returned, was said to have four or five children there by another wife. Her siblings had children – the youngest sister, aged only 22, already had three boys and a girl.

For Miriam, to be 'her age' and childless was a terrible dishonour.

Amazingly, almost all the time before John sounded the Peugeot's horn in the road on the other side of the house, with a brief intermission while she made me more coffee and found some shortbread, passed in discussion of this grief and shame of Miriam's. I talked, for instance, about relatives and friends in Britain who had adopted children. Might that be the answer?

Her face setting even deeper in sorrow, Miriam thought not. After an hour she seemed desperate, not the composed hostess of last

254

night, but a woman distraught, in deep pain. I resisted the impulse to hug her, squeeze her. My last remarks before I collected my case and headed for the car concerned a cousin of mine who, childless, at last had adopted a boy and a girl. The dam, so to speak, had broken, and her own daughter had soon followed...

"Good luck!" I cried.

"Thank you," she said simply and softly, wiping her face before confronting John.

He saw her raise a hand weakly in farewell at her door.

"Fine woman, that," he remarked, salaciously. "But she have no children." He changed into top gear, the wide empty road beckoned. The skies were grey again. "And no black man can give her a child."

John, though his uniform was barely less tidy, had a whiff of the shebeen about him. His driving remained accurate, however, while the point of what he had said sank into my returning depression.

The gossip in the town. Robert sterile, if not impotent. A laughing stock, perhaps. Robert leaving for work so early. Was he compliant in a scheme of hers? Though they were obviously serious churchgoers, with works of popular theology dominating their bookcase, they were not manically pious. In any case, the antinomian heresy had always served Christians well when their carnal cravings became irresistible.

The vacancy left by the spider's body, the void in Miriam's womb, were completely unrelated, but I always remember them together.

Years later, in a University Common Room, I met a fellow 'Old African Hand' who knew the college I'd visited so briefly, had spent a week or two there in the mid eighties. I wondered if the Cartwrights by then had acquired a flock of adopted bairns, but he could remember no Cartwrights.

What he did remember vividly, he said, was the outrageousness of the prostitutes in the nearby town, flaunting themselves in despite of the puritanical (hypocritical) ideology of the regime, which banned miniskirts. AIDS had just come to the fore when he was there. Now the whole country was swamped in it.

"Shame," he said. "Beautiful country. Lovely people." I thought: grey skies, sometimes. And a lonely, distressed woman half-infatuated with Jacob, who was himself wholly infatuated with football and jam.

Let's Be Frank

By Eoin Sanders

I had gone to bed the previous night the same
way I always did; dazed and confused. I'd
been trying to make some sense of Carl Jung's
babblings and had finally called the whole thing
off and returned to George MacDonald Fraser's
Flashman before deciding somewhere around
two that I really should call it a night. There was,
as you can see, nothing to indicate that anything
at all out of the ordinary was in the offing.

And yet, just before 7 o'clock in the morning,
something very much out of the ordinary but
very much in keeping with my penchant for
drama did happen. A blood clot chose that
moment to break free somewhere and, after
wending its way through my circulatory system,
it lodged in my left frontal lobe. At 6:53am I
stroked out.

Of course, I didn't know it was a stroke at the
time. As far as my mangled brain recalls it – and
I don't think it will ever become clearer than
snapshot images and shattered fragments of
half-imagined scenes – I was having something
of a nightmare and had woken up to find the roof
of my mouth unbearably itchy. I was feverishly
using my tongue to scratch it and becoming
aware that something was not quite right. It was
while trying to shake off the last of sleep and
thinking that I was lucid dreaming that I decided
to stand up. Bad move.

My wife, it must be said, remembers things
rather differently. Indeed, she recalls being
woken up by an unearthly combination of grunts
and yowls as well as weapons-grade twitching.

I am no stranger to night terrors and she knows the drill so shook me and fairly gently asked me what the matter was. When no real response came, she turned over and attempted to go back to sleep.

It was then that I attempted to get to my feet. It was then that I discovered that the right side of my body was paralysed and it was very shortly afterwards that I went careering head first into the wall and latterly the laundry bins. Later yet, though only seconds so, we both realised – though with different levels of understanding – that something was terribly wrong.

From my position on the floor I was vaguely aware of my other half leaping out of bed and declaring with remarkable calm, "I think you've had a stroke" before bolting from the room. For my part I was still struggling with the fall/wall/floor conundrum and not getting very far. When my brain finally caught the gist of her words I thought them simply preposterous and on the heels of that came, "I am not getting in any ambulance in these pants".

The following minutes are jumbled and, when stitched together, show that I lost consciousness several times before the ambulance arrived – I wasn't, for instance, aware that she had phoned 999 a second time when no paramedics had arrived some 15 minutes after the first call. But the bits that are there make for much amusement when recounted. That is to say; I find them funny, others seem less amused and she in particular does not seem to enjoy the retelling at all.

Maybe it's uncomfortable for her because she has never seen me so truly helpless as I was then; scrabbling around half crippled and pathetically attempting to pull a t-shirt on with my one good hand because I didn't want the ambulance crew · to see me in only my Homer Simpson boxer shorts. Maybe I find it funny because, at that stage, the whole affair was in no way traumatic for me. I couldn't make head nor tail of events so my memories, such as they are, are tainted with an air of unreality and detachment. For my wife it was all too real. Or maybe it's actually that it truly did terrify me and I'm covering up my emotional inability to deal with the recollections by laughing at them. There is a slim chance that it's actually funny, but I've been wrong about bad taste jokes before.

Of course, another possibility springs to mind. But it's one I don't like thinking about. In fact, it's with some trepidation that I tiptoe round the issue... but I can't help thinking that Frank might have turned up. And, putting it mildly, Frank's not right.

I can hear your confusion, so an explanation is in order.

For a long time I called him 'The Other' in an attempt to distance myself from the malignant and vengeful freak. But over the years I came to learn that there's more to him than that and so he gained a name.

He is, essentially, me but with... differences. Frank's personality has tattoos and even his eyes have teeth. The man is an unhinged maniac. Everything that terrifies me, Frank seems to enjoy. The more I'm going to pieces the closer he comes to breaking through. And when he comes through... well... I won't go into it but there are reasons why I've moved about the country a fair bit. I won't make jokes about knowing where the bodies are buried because I don't. Frank does.

Don't get me wrong, Frank isn't all bad – not quite. His fearlessness has saved me more than once and his humour has pulled me through some dark times. That's another thing that makes me think he showed up that day. You see, early on my first morning in hospital, still addled, still paralysed and still virtually speechless, I looked at my wife (who was watching me closely, as you can imagine) and slurred the first totally coherent sentence since my brain fused.

"This happened because I make fun of cripples, didn't it?" I said. Then I sniggered and I really can't say that I sounded like myself. At the time, well, I thought the reasons for that were obvious, but now I'm not so sure.

Now that I think of it, there were other signs that Frank was there too – sudden hot thoughts and dark intentions. But the thing that has suddenly begun to worry me the most is that I can't remember him leaving.

And now that I look back, I notice that my recent liking for late night walks in sad, dark places began around the time of my release from hospital. I'd been telling myself it was a phase, but...

The dreams I've been having recently of cold hands digging holes and heavy carpet-wrapped lumps are starting to ring bells more associated with memory than with nightmares.

People have been saying my mood is getting darker. My laugh is getting coarser and, all of sudden, it's beginning to feel like my eyes have teeth.

And now, now I'm terrified that I didn't survive that morning. Someone else did.

Stop This Shit Now!

By Peter Burnett

That's right, the year is 2008 and Edinburgh's nature is fractured and dual. At least, according to the writers, academics and critics (WACs) that have been telling us this. From their warm, gadget filled studies, these WACs have been concocting a fantasy about the miraculous and mind-blowing duality of our lovely city.

YOUNG OFFENDERS

It all became too much when Irvine Welsh stunned audiences of the South Bank Show with the staggering revelation that Edinburgh was a divided city. Sitting in a bar he used to ken, Welsh told Melvyn Bragg about how Edinburgh was uniquely divided into Old Town, ken, and New Town, ken, which was a metaphor for the whole thing like. This was accompanied with much twattish muttering on Jekyll and Hyde, Burke and Hare, James Hogg and OH NO HE COULDN'T THINK OF ANY OTHER EXAMPLES and that was about it.

IAN

Then Ian Rankin swooped, presenting Hidden Edinburgh on BBC4, in which he attacked the same cliché with glee. Viewers were shocked when Ian stepped to camera to ask: "What are the roots of the split in Edinburgh's nature?" After much of the usual rigmarole about Burke and Hare, Jekyll and Hyde and twatting in the Old Town and the New Town, Rankin came up with the genius conclusion: "The city's division goes a lot deeper than between rich and poor." Stop this shit now!

MINGERS

Next, Hidden Edinburgh turned on the brothel at 17 Danube Street. According to the show, "Edinburgh also has a dual attitude towards sex." Stop this shit now! We were enjoying that bit about the brothel, and revelling in the photography of one of Edinburgh's most attractive neo-Greek streets, with its crescent and grand centrepiece. And all we got was more cow-crud about Edinburgh's supposed dual nature. No! Then Edinburgh's committee for the Six Cities Festival exhibition picked up the baton. "Edinburgh has a schizophrenic nature, caught between the rational and the irrational, nostalgia and modernity, the urban and the natural," they said. Stop this shit now! It's unbearable. Duality and the divided mind have been a source of fascination for literary artists in other places for a long time now, and we don't just mean Glasgow and Aberdeen, you mingers.

EXPLOSION

The action heated up in August last year at the Book Festival in Charlotte Square Gardens, when in a discussion on the Armenian genocide of 1915, Taner Akçam talked of the duality of the Turkish nation, which he suggested has "different subcultures, and different collective memories." Later Akçam was accused of stealing Edinburgh's thunder and was shown to the massive Gothic spire of the Sir Walter Scott Monument and asked to climb the 287 narrow and winding steps to the top and take in the view of the city, where below him, enshrined in the open vault was the seated statue of Sir Walter Scott dressed in a border plaid and accompanied by his favourite deer-hound Maida, all carved from a lovely 30 ton block of Carara marble. Akçam was implored to recognise the duality of

Edinburgh, but instead he chose to talk about the Armenian genocide of 1915. WACs were shocked.

ASK NO QUESTIONS

In case you are a WAC and are still spouting this twattish cattle-crap about Edinburgh's dual nature, here's a quick quiz which you should repeat until you get all the answers right:

1. Who wrote The Double?
a) Robert Louis Stevenson
b) Deacon Brodie
c) Louise Welsh
d) None of the above

2. The opposition and combination of the universe's two basic principles of yin and yang is a large part of which religion?
a) Presbyterianism
b) Taoism
c) Orangeism

3. In his study The Double in Nineteenth-Century Fiction, John Herdman concluded what?
a) That although William Godwin, Charles Brockden Brown, ETA Hoffman, James Hogg, Gogol, Dostoyevsky, Stevenson, Wilde, Kipling, Maupassant, Poe and Chekhov all employed doubles in their fiction, it was only Hogg and Stevenson that really mattered.
b) That although all of the above writers explored the self-division inherent in the doppelganger figure and were influenced by a wider Gothic tradition, all their ideas were in my opinion stolen from Edinburgh.
c) That if you mention Edinburgh's dual nature in an interview, you might look as if you had read something other than Harry Potter.

263

4. You are an up and coming WAC and asked to comment on the novel Kidnapped by Robert Louis Stevenson. What do you say?
a) That Jamie Bell should definitely play David.
b) That Kidnapped really demonstrates the dual nature in Edinburgh.
c) "Oooh, see that Alan Breck Stewart, he's got a real Jekyll and Hyde personality."

5. Paris, Lisbon and Berlin are all beautiful European capitals. But which major tourist attraction do they all seriously lack?
a) Greggses
b) Deacon Brodie's pub
c) A dual nature, obviously.

For more on Edinburgh's dual nature, go to www.whatacrockofshite.com and click on STOP THIS SHIT NOW!

Next time: Only Three Glasgows – Triple Personality on the West Coast. Peter Burnett is a writer, academic, novelist and critic. In short, a WANC.

The Fetch Goes

By Raymond Bell

Sometimes I wonder about the death of ghosts.
As Francis Thompson wrote in Ghosts, Spirits
and Spectres of Scotland, the ghosts of the living
once outnumbered the spirits of the dead in this
country, although few are aware of that now.

Formerly, such entities were to be found
not just stalking their victims, but stealing
their identities. They did not bother with the
pretence of the grave. Now they pass their time
by attacking groups of tourists in Greyfriars
Kirkyard, and offering platitudes to the bereaved
of the Morrison Street Spiritualist congregation.

Such doppelgangers were known as 'fetches'
here. According to Rev Kirk's The Secret
Commonwealth, a fetch is 'Reflex man, a Co-
Walker, every way like the Man, as a Twin-
brother and companion, haunting him as his
shadow, as is oft seen and known among Men
(resembling the Originall), both before and after
the Originall is dead'. In Gaelic, a fetch was
known as a samhladh, which translates literally
as 'likeness' or 'copy'.

Fetches probably got their name from delivering
people to Hades, Valhalla or wherever they were
going. They were human anti-matter. I have
no idea whether each individual got allotted a
personal wraith, or whether a multipurpose fetch
performed the same function for several people.
Suffice to say, they were reportedly very good at
pretending to be other people, and fooled many.
They were never considered healthy things, or
a topic for post-prandial conversation, for they
were the precursors of certain death.

It is difficult to argue that such things, which lacked an independent existence, could die by themselves. Death or no death, the double is always a parasitic outgrowth. If it survives its host's death, then it becomes emptier as a result, for it can only copy what was, not what is, or will be.

Even in the day of Robert Louis Stevenson, the fetch was in terminal decline. I believe that Jekyll And Hyde was an unsuitable title, because Jekyll is Hyde. Hyde is neither the double, nor opposite of Jekyll. Like north and south, Jekyll and Hyde form an artificial division of a single body, with no gap between them. The pun on 'hide' is probably intentional: Jekyll evades his hypocrisy through substance abuse. Likewise, Confessions Of A Justified Sinner describes delusion, not duality. It is doubtful if Gilmartin exists in his own right.

And this is it – it is all too easy to let yourself off the hook through so-called 'duality'. For example, if you are a famous crime writer, and want to make a statement, you can make it through your detective alter ego, but if the statement proves to be unpopular, you can disown it and ascribe it to him alone. I do have some personal experience of this technique, although in my case, I was still at nursery school, and much less successful with it. "The other Raymond did it," I would say, but the teachers and my parents would have none of it. The phase did not last long, as my evil twin fled in terror of retribution. In the old days, they would not have blamed such behaviour on parents, teachers or a bad diet – I would have been a 'changeling', a replica child dumped on unsuspecting mortals. I never did get to meet that other Raymond, and I suspect that probably I am him.

The ghost of the past dichotomy is still channelled by pseuds and commissars; for example, why talk of the Old and New Town, when Edinburgh has at least a dozen other districts? She has evolved radically within our lifetimes. She has gone from twin town to boom town, but some prefer to see her as the land of the dead. Doublethink persists in some quarters, and while it is true that there are some residents who maintain a pallid version of Glaswegian bigotry, and some provincials who try and replicate London high society, they do not reflect the majority. Edinburgh now contends with an overarching American cultural dominance and a European polity in addition to her Scottish and British facets. Edinburgh is once again a proper capital, and there are no two ways about it. The worst of Manichaeism is past, and John Knox is unfashionable in the modern Kirk.

The City of Literature crew has recently spawned one of Edinburgh's outstanding examples of contemporary horror, namely its attempts to get more people reading. On the surface, they were successful, and brought kudos to the council which subsidised them. Thousands of free copies of Kidnapped and Jekyll and Hyde were distributed, nearly all in libraries and schools. Personally, I cannot think of a dafter idea, as not only is this the way to spend vast amounts of public money, but also how to pick up absolutely no new readers. This is because most people learn to despise literature in the classroom, and those who escape from there unscathed tend to use the libraries anyway. Giving away books in a library is a bit like advertising cigarettes in a tobacconist.

It is not as if Robert Louis Stevenson's books are that hard to come by, or particularly expensive, but conveniently, he happens to be dead. As a substitute for supporting the city's contemporary writers, we get copies (samhlaidhean) and adaptations of his work. He's not about to complain, or misbehave himself, by becoming a junkie or jakie, or upset members of the concerned public by making controversial statements about independence or praising Margaret Thatcher, as Irvine Welsh is alleged to do.

The so called Scottish Enlightenment is a big industry these days, and is another fallback for those who see themselves as guardians of Edinburgh's culture. It is the wellspring of an imagined modern dualism. But the Enlightenment industry is blind to the political and social conditions prevailing when Hume and Hutton were at their height – the aftershocks of the French Revolution were rippling through the slums, which were already beginning to fill with evicted peasants. From the top of the North Bridge, one not only sees the elaborate Scott Monument, but an unassuming needle in Calton Cemetery dedicated to Thomas Muir of Huntershill, both covered in soot. At this point, free thought and radicalism were generally tolerated in science, toned down in architecture, and in politics, repaid with deportation to a penal colony. It was the time of Lord Braxfield, an early representative of the Lanarkshire mafia, and a medieval throwback. Better not be possessed by the geist of the Scottish Enlightenment.

In contemporary politics, the double has also tended to make way for the dead. An extreme example would be Adam Lyall who, each election, advertises his business by standing for the Witchery Tour Party. Unlike many other regional list candidates, Lyall is at least honest enough to admit he doesn't have much life in him, for he stole his name from a dead man.

The internal contradiction could power
Stevenson and Hogg, but it was ultimately a
cancer. Seemingly, neither of them praised it,
or wished it to endure. Hugh MacDiarmid could
have made more out of it, but his 'antisyzygy'
is at least a gift to desperate Scrabble players.
There is a great danger that comes from those
haunted by its spectre, for they prefer the dead
cliché over the living reality. Like a bad dream, it
lingers on, but only half remembered.

Above: Lucy's cover illustration for Number 17
says it all.

Duality: Come In, Your Time Is Up

By Kevin Williamson

If 'duality' is such a popular number, where are all
the songs? The only one that springs to mind is
Duality by Slipknot. It begins 'I push my fingers
into my eyes.' Slipknot are a band who wear
black-and-white masks on stage. Presumably
because their eyes are sore.

'Duality' fares little better on the big screen, or,
for that matter, on the glass nipple. The nearest
we have is an old episode of Alexei Sayle's Stuff
called Cartesian Dualism For The Fuller Figure,
starring Alexei Sayle, naturally, and Doris Hare.
(Alexei Sayle was the landlord in The Young
Ones. Doris Hare was Stan's mother in On The
Buses.)

Sayle and Hare – the yin and yang of English
comedy – do their best, but if references to duality
are an indicator of its cultural pre-eminence then
we should really be seeing it everywhere.

Old school duality – or Duality 1.0 – is the
foundation on which western culture has been
built. Good guys versus bad guys, darkness
versus light, where never the twain shall meet.
This simplistic primal stuff is personified in
the Old Testament (written around 900BC)
but probably goes much further back into our
prehistory. Darkness equals the unknown equals
danger and fear. It just needs horns and a tail
and hey presto!

Duality 1.0 has ruled the roost for almost all of
recorded history. It still does.

You can observe it in the ongoing George Bush/ Osama bin Laden narrative. It's crude stuff, straight out of a Hollywood western, but I guess these guys like it uncomplicated. Someone should have told them that when two card players hold the same hand, neither is going to win. They should have just split the pot and saved everyone's time.

Scotland has been a natural environment for duality to take root in, what with all those Scottish/ British, Highlands/Lowlands, Gaelic/English dichotomies spinning around in our heads.

Although Scots can't claim to have invented duality – unlike tar macadam, hypodermic needles, cloned sheep and the telly – if you listened to Scotland's criticatti waffling on about it, you'd think it was our cultural equivalent of Einstein's theory of relativity.

Scotland's great love affair with duality stretches back to when the Catholic Church showed great ingenuity in its methods of torturing and killing people who showed symptoms of batting for the other side. Symptoms such as having a stutter. Or, in the case of women and gays, liking the cock.

When the Catholic Church ran out of thumbscrews and popular support, John Boy Knox and his followers stepped up to the holy plate. Anything the Papes could do the Prods could do better. From 1560 onwards there was much a-screaming, a-burning and a-dunking as the Reformation danced its merry jig. Good and evil remained mutually exclusive and the One True Faithers were the very chaps to tell ain fi the ither.

Then, on Christmas Eve, 1696, came one of those pivotal moments in history that didn't seem much to begin with. Like when Archduke Franz

Ferdinand was shot in 1914. Or when Don Masson missed that penalty against Peru.

Thomas Aikenhead, an 18 year old student at Edinburgh University (this was in a bygone age when Edinburgh University allowed Scots to study there) decided to add to the list of Scottish inventions. He came up with the first ever rag week. His college jape was to say religion was all pish and we were all Donald Ducked when we died.

Oh, how the Presbyterian elders laughed at young Aikenhead's jest. They chuckled and they chuckled. All the way to a hangman's noose erected near the top of Leith Walk.

To his eternal credit, Aikenhead stuck to his guns. As the rope was made ready, he read out a statement saying that he doubted the objectivity of good and evil, and that moral laws were the work of governments or men. This was revolutionary stuff that challenged the hegemony of Duality 1.0. Alas, this was no solace to oor Tam, as the fundamentalist thought-police kicked the platform from under his feet.

After that unholy episode, and the ruckus that followed it, the tight Presbyterian grip on our nation's throat loosened. The theocratic Taliban who ruled Scotland were put on the back foot and a new enlightened version of duality would be plucked from this Calvanistic quagmire. Duality 2.0. Where darkness shone bright in the saintly soul of all mortals. And vice versa.

James Hogg's Memoirs and Confessions Of A Justified Sinner and Robert Louis Stevenson's The Strange Case Of Dr Jekyll And Mr Hyde are the literary rabbits routinely pulled from the hat to say: "See, Ah telt ye."

James Hogg set the scene with his aforementioned religious thriller, in which nothing is quite what it seems. But it was Robert Louis Stevenson's malevolent classic, set in the fog-enshrouded back streets of Victorian London/Edinburgh, that most famously articulated the concept.

Duality got personal. A doctor by day. A cocaine fiend by night. The polar extremes of Duality 1.0 gradually come together. The division between the good doctor and his evil alter ego blurs. In this sense, Edward Hyde is more of a merger than a takeover.

Stevenson's 'shilling shocker' – as it was called at the time – was published in 1886. This was the same year that Coca-Cola launched a brown fizzy drink whose secret ingredient was cocaine.

(Note to the Coca-Cola Corporation: How about putting the genie back in the bottle? Just for a laugh. It would seriously screw with the international prohibition racket, as well as being a poke in the eye for Pepsi. Just a thought.)

The story of Jekyll and Hyde is your typical chemical romance. Man gets curious. Man discovers white powders. Man falls in love. Kaboom! Or as Henry Jekyll puts it:

'There was something strange in my sensations, something indescribably new and, from its very novelty, incredibly sweet. I felt younger, lighter, happier in body; within I was conscious of a heady recklessness, a current of disordered sensual images running like a mill-race in my fancy, a solution of the bonds of obligation, an unknown but not innocent freedom of the soul. I knew myself, at the first breath of this new life, to be more wicked, tenfold more wicked, sold a slave to my original evil; and the thought, in that moment, braced and delighted me like wine.'

In a nutshell, the good doctor was getting cunted. And loving every minute of it. Some readers may be familiar with the premise of this cautionary tale. "Been there. Done it. Got the Alabama 3 T-shirt."

Contrary to Hollywood mythology, in the RLS book there are no foaming test-tubes, nor are there any hairy makeovers. The white powders – for that is how they are described – prise open Jekyll's doors of perception and arouse his senses. The doctor would soon be deliberating morosely on the nature of identity and personality.

RLS was on to something. Through the character of Henry Jekyll, in the most lucid visionary mind-blowing chapter of his great novel, Stevenson reflects on the duality of man. This is the confessionary Chapter Ten, entitled Henry Jekyll's Full Statement Of The Case. (This chapter still contains the earliest and best descriptions of the effects of cocaine in all English literature).

As Henry Jekyll gets wired into the snarf, a growing realisation makes itself felt:

'With every day, and from both sides of my intelligence, the moral and the intellectual, I thus drew steadily nearer to that truth, by whose partial discovery I have been doomed to such a dreadful shipwreck: that man is not truly one, but truly two... I for my part, from the nature of my life, advanced infallibly in one direction and in one direction only. It was on the moral side, and in my own person, that I learned to recognise the thorough and primitive duality of man.'

In the arena of literature, Stevenson was probing deeper into the complexities of the human mind, personality and identity than science had thus far investigated. Psychoanalysis, mindfucks, and the ubiquitous sofa had not yet been invented. And for good reason, because Sigmund Freud was also out his tree on gak.

Two years before RLS wrote Jekyll And Hyde Freud published a paper called On Coca. Freud had become bored with the possibilities of nitrous oxide – laughing-gas parties were all the rage back then – and had zoned in on cocaine for its transformative and medical qualities. He fell in love with his 'magical substance' and evangelically declared that cocaine was the new wonder-drug. He concluded, none too wisely: 'A first dose, or even repeated doses, of coca produce no compulsive desire to use the stimulant further.'

At this point in the mid-1880s, Freud and Stevenson were fellow-travellers, although I have not seen any evidence that either was familiar with the other's work. But, through their chosen fields of creative endeavour, both were encouraging further investigation into the workings of the human mind.

Freud's investigations would go far beyond the mere intersection of good and evil. He would lay down the basis for a new science in which Duality 2.0 would gradually be replaced by multiplicity, and the interaction of the conscious and the subconscious.

To gauge how revolutionary these 19th century writers were, we shouldn't forget that even now, in 2008, when an abominable crime takes place, followed by much wailing and gnashing of teeth, it is on the medieval precepts of Duality 1.0 that newspapers and commentators often fall back.

I'll conclude with this thought. Much as
Stevenson's Jekyll And Hyde is routinely
described as 'the duality novel' par excellence, is it
possible that RLS was a visionary who anticipated
that the concept of Duality 2.0 would quickly
become dated and surpassed as an understanding
of the human mind grew?

To return to that quote from Henry Jekyll which
begins 'With every day... ' Half way through it
I use a quotation device called 'three wee dots'.
These are used to indicate that part of the text has
been edited out, usually for brevity.

And now, dear readers (as they used to say) here
are the two sentences I surreptitiously edited out
of that quote and replaced with the three wee
dots. These forty-eight words are the ones usually
overlooked when the criticatti hold forth on the
subject of Robert Louis Stevenson, Jekyll And
Hyde and duality:

'I say two, because the state of my own knowledge
does not pass beyond that point. Others will
follow, others will outstrip me on the same lines;
and I hazard the guess that man will be ultimately
known for a mere polity of multifarious,
incongruous and independent denizens.'

Despite his gothic associations, I like to think
that if Robert Louis Stevenson were alive today,
walking through Edinburgh's Old Town on his
way to Rutherford's Bar, the tune he'd have
playing on his iPod wouldn't be Slipknot's Duality.
Perhaps it would be something more like Bitter
Sweet Symphony by the Verve.

I am here in my mold
and I'm a million different people
from one day to the next...

Appendix

A User's Guide To The One O'clock Gun

By Lucy McKenzie

FIG 1. Educated solitary drinker eyes the Gun in its box, a familiar sight in all first-rate Edina taverns.

FIG 2. Curious, he plucks the current issue from the box and eyes it speculatively.

FIGS 3a & b. He delights in the ingenious folds and embarks upon a literary odyssey.

FIG 4. His delight increases as he realises he is in fact holding a double sided A2 broadsheet, packed with stories, poems and art.

FIG 5. Hooked, having devoured the front page, he feverishly turns it around to feast upon the back.

Fɪɢ 6. The Gun conveniently pocketed, he spreads the word among his fellow topers.

Solution To The Spot-The-Stereotype Challenge (from page 211)

How did you score?

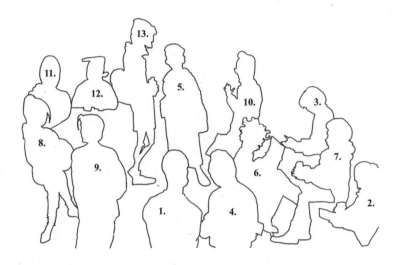

1. Working Class Hero ('77 Punk Poet)
2. Scottish Renaissance Man
3. Edinburgh Literati
4. Edinburgh Underground Literati
5. Mature Student (Ex-Stevenson/Telford)
6. Intellectual Coffee-drinker
7. Gallerist In A Hat
8. Easy Art Student (Bright Young Thing)
9. Lecherous College Tutor
10. Ex-Smiths Fan
11. Cynical Barmaid
12. Embittered Pub Bore
13. New Town Eccentric

Index of Writers

One O'Clock Gun Anthology ISBN 978-0-9554885-5-9

First published 2010 by Leamington Books Ltd
53 Bothwell Street, Glasgow, G2 6TS.

A CIP record for this book is available from the BL and NLS.